She couldn't [...]
including No [...]
happened too [...]

"I kind of wanted to cut down a tree for you and the girls the way your dad did," Noah said.

No, no, no. Don't say something romantic!

"I didn't grow up with that experience," he continued. "We had a fake tree and store-bought decorations."

"Okay, let's find ourselves a tree." Hannah pushed the stroller past him until his hand covered hers, strong and firm. *Breathe, Hannah, breathe.* She did...and inhaled his fresh, woodsy scent. Almost pine, but not quite. Whatever it was, it was raw and intoxicating.

"Allow me." His lips were so close, her hair moved as he spoke.

She gripped the stroller tighter for fear if she let go she'd melt into a puddle. *This can't be happening.*

She wasn't permitted to think of Noah as anyone other than Charlotte and Cheyenne's father. She was in trouble. Being around him heightened her senses and left her feeling very protected at the same time. She didn't need to feel protected. She could take care of herself. She could take care of the girls herself, the same way Lauren had.

But she didn't want to. God help her, she didn't want to do it without Noah...

Dear Reader,

I had a very clear image of Clay Tanner's sister, Hannah, when I wrote *A Texan for Hire* last year. Even though she had a very small part in that book, every time I closed my eyes, the opening scenes from *Twins for Christmas* played out before me. Whenever I drove past an old farmhouse, I envisioned her and Noah standing on the front porch with two little faces peering through the screen door behind them. Finally, one afternoon I sat down and wrote the entire synopsis in under three hours. While it was the easiest proposal I've written, the same couldn't be said about the book. It was the hardest to date. The emotional backdrop of this story broke my heart. I wanted to reach through my computer and wrap my arms around Charlotte and Cheyenne—the eighteen-month-old twins featured in this story. A huge part of me fell in love with this family, and someday I'll revisit the girls as they grow older.

Twins for Christmas is the ninth book in the Welcome to Ramblewood series...where the door is always open.

Feel free to stop in and visit me at amandarenee.com. I'd love to hear from you. Happy reading!

Amanda Renee

TWINS FOR CHRISTMAS

—

AMANDA RENEE

HARLEQUIN® WESTERN ROMANCE®

Recycling programs
for this product may
not exist in your area.

ISBN-13: 978-0-373-75740-4

Twins for Christmas

Printed in U.S.A.

Amanda Renee was raised in the Northeast and now wriggles her toes in the warm coastal Carolina sands. Her career began when she was discovered through Harlequin's So You Think You Can Write contest. When not creating stories about love and laughter, she enjoys the company of her schnoodle, Duffy, camping, playing guitar and piano, photography, and anything involving horses. You can visit her at amandarenee.com.

Books by Amanda Renee

Harlequin American Romance

Welcome to Ramblewood

Betting on Texas
Home to the Cowboy
Blame It on the Rodeo
A Texan for Hire
Back to Texas
Mistletoe Rodeo
The Trouble with Cowgirls
A Bull Rider's Pride

Visit the Author Profile page
at Harlequin.com for more titles.

Anna
For all the laughter, wails
and puppy dog tales.
Thank you for being my friend,
proofreader and sanity keeper.

Chapter One

Noah Knight's wet jeans clung uncomfortably to his thighs. Drenched, he took refuge from the rain in a dimly lit bar. Finnegan's Pub in College Station, Texas, catered to an older crowd. At thirty-two he wasn't exactly middle-aged, but he was too old to find common ground with the majority of the local college students.

Once, sometimes twice, a year he conducted helicopter-logging recruitment seminars in town. Now he had four hours until his flight home to Aurora, Oregon. It gave him enough time to grab a bite and a beer or two before catching a cab to the airport. Noah wanted a booth to himself, but they were all taken, so he sat at the bar. He wasn't in the mood for company after being awake for the last thirty hours.

He placed his order and reviewed the preliminary applications he'd collected during the seminar. One out of the twelve had potential, while the rest had been drawn to the danger of the job rather than the job itself.

"Enough work for today," Noah muttered. He flipped his portfolio closed and jammed it into his bag, then picked up the folded newspaper someone had left behind on the stool next to him.

"That poor girl." The bartender nodded to the paper as he set a pint of beer on a coaster in front of Noah. "She used to come in here and study right over there in that booth." He nodded toward the corner of the pub. "Said it was quieter than the sorority house. Lived on coffee and fries."

Noah read the obituary.

Lauren Marie Elgrove, 24, Boston, Massachusetts, formerly of Ramblewood, Texas, was killed Friday, November 18, 2016, in a car accident. Born on October 30, 1992, to James and Elizabeth Elgrove (both deceased) of San Angelo, Texas. She is survived by her twin twenty-one-month-old daughters, Charlotte and Cheyenne. Graveside services will be held at 10:00 a.m. on Tuesday at the Memorial Garden Cemetery. In lieu of flowers, contributions to the Charlotte and Cheyenne Education Fund are being accepted through Hannah Tanner of Ramblewood.

Noah felt a touch of sadness. A single cold paragraph seemed inappropriate when someone's life had been cut so short. He unfolded the newspaper and the woman in the photograph above the obituary almost knocked him off his stool. Carefully he read the caption: "Lauren Elgrove with her daughters, Charlotte and Cheyenne."

Lauren. His shoulders sagged. They'd met a few years ago in this very bar. She had graduated earlier that day and had been celebrating with a friend. The memory made him smile. He had found her fascinating as she spoke of biochemistry and physics. He could still hear her infectious laugh. They'd spent the night together tangled between the sheets, but he woke up the following morning alone.

Last names and phone numbers had been an afterthought and he'd never seen her again, which was a shame because he had wanted a chance to get to know her better. She'd popped into his head a few times since then, probably more than he cared to admit.

He calculated the dates quickly in his head—they'd slept together around two and a half years ago. Staring at the photograph, he saw his own eyes reflected back in the twins' faces. Noah's chest tightened and he swore he stopped breathing. Was it possible? Were Charlotte and Cheyenne his daughters? His gut told him he already knew the answer, but he needed confirmation.

His mind raced. "Excuse me." Noah fought to steady his voice and waved for the bartender. "You—" He cleared his throat as the man approached. "You said you knew this woman—Lauren Elgrove?"

The bartender's head slowly bobbed up and down. "She had a bright future ahead of her."

"There's no mention of the children's father. Do they have one?" Noah winced at his own question. Nervousness trumped diplomacy and tact. The sinking feeling in the pit of his stomach told him he was the father.

"I haven't seen Lauren in at least two years." The bartender shrugged. "I didn't even know she had kids until I saw her obituary. Your order will be right up."

Noah attempted to wrap his mind around the possibility he'd fathered twins without knowing it. What were the chances? If she had spent the night with him, maybe she had done the same thing with other men. That didn't seem like Lauren. Not that he knew who Lauren had really been. One night certainly hadn't made him an expert. Despite the passion they'd shared, there had been a shyness about her and he doubted she'd slept around.

He raked his fingers down his face and exhaled. How could it be possible? They had used protection. Picking up the paper again, he braved another glance at the photo. His hands shook as he scanned the grainy print. Speculating wouldn't do him any good. He needed to physically lay eyes on them and see for himself.

Noah smacked the top of the bar. "Change of plans. Make mine to go and can you call me a taxi?" Home would have to wait. Instead, he intended to rent a car and drive to the town mentioned in the newspaper. Ramblewood, wherever that was. He wasn't leaving the state until he found out if those girls were his. His head began to spin. What if they were his daughters? Did he want to be their father?

FOR THE SECOND night in a row, Hannah Tanner paced the floor of the twins' bedroom. She cradled one girl in each arm in an attempt to soothe them. It had been less than a week since Lauren's death. She hadn't yet processed that she'd never see her best friend again, let alone that she was the legal guardian of twins.

"Mommy!" Cheyenne shrieked at the top of her

lungs. The girls had been restless last night, but tonight was much worse. She'd been adamantly against letting them attend Lauren's funeral earlier in the day, but her family had convinced her the children needed some semblance of closure and a chance to say goodbye. She didn't feel they needed to see the coffin or know Mommy was going in the ground. She shivered at the thought. She understood death, but it was Lauren. How could she be gone?

The twins were having a hard time adjusting to the drastic changes in their lives and she couldn't blame them. It had been bad enough when Lauren accepted a job so far away, moving her small family to Boston. Now the children were uprooted once again. Hannah couldn't remember anything that had occurred in her life at twenty-one months old and she hoped the girls would forget both the upheaval and the funeral this morning. But doing so would mean they'd forget their mother, and Hannah couldn't bear the thought.

"What's a matter, baby girl?" Her sister-in-law, Abby, entered the room and lifted Cheyenne out of her arms. "Hannah, why don't you take a shower and unwind for a little bit. I'm not going anywhere. You need a break."

The strength to protest escaped her, which would have been fine if her heart didn't fill with guilt every time the girls were out of sight. They were perceptive and they knew something was wrong. Her mother said they were grieving. How was that possible if they didn't understand the concept of never seeing their mother again? No, they were confused. They'd been in a horrific car accident and now Mommy wasn't around.

Hannah padded down the hallway into the bathroom, closing the door and shutting herself off from the rest of the world. She could still hear the officer explaining what had happened. Lauren had been thrown from the car and had died on impact. Thankfully, the twins had been relatively unharmed. Hannah had caught a flight to Boston the following morning to pick up the girls, her mother by her side. Monday morning, the four of them had flown home to Ramblewood. The funeral home had arranged for Lauren to be flown back with them.

Everything had happened so fast. Thanksgiving was in two days. The twins' second Thanksgiving and the first without their mother. And then there was Christmas. How would they ever get through Christmas? *How would they get through today?*

After her shower, she peeked in the room at Charlotte and Cheyenne. Both twins were curled up together in one crib while Abby read them a bedtime story. She tiptoed down the stairs, praying the worn boards wouldn't creak and shift the twins' focus from Abby onto her. Her belly growled. It had been days since she'd last eaten a decent meal.

Trays of food covered the butcher-block kitchen countertop. She had intended to sand and oil the counter this week as part of her never-ending house renovations. It'd have to wait along with the rest of her plans. She grabbed a plate from the cupboard and lifted the foil lids of various dishes.

"Honey, I didn't hear you come down." Her mother appeared in the doorway. "I've devised a system. Desserts not needing refrigeration are on this counter." Fern waved her arm dramatically as if she were Vanna White turning a letter. "The other nonperishables, like breads and crackers, are over here. And I managed to freeze most of the casseroles, but I left the sandwiches and salads in the refrigerator for you to nibble on. What wouldn't fit in your freezer, your father took home to ours. Let us know when you need something and we'll send it over."

"I think we have enough food to last a year." Hannah chose a turkey sandwich, poured herself a glass of water and sat at the table. "Mom, how am I going to afford this? Most of my money goes into the ranch. I still have upcoming competitions I'd be crazy to back out of. We need the prize money. It helps that I board and train horses, but it's still not enough for the three of us to live off. I can't compete in Vegas in a few weeks with all this going on. I'd pick up some extra hours teaching at the rodeo school if I had any extra hours to give." She shook her head. "That would mean spending less time with the girls, and I won't do that to them. I still can't believe Lauren didn't have life insurance."

Fern sat across from her at the table, clasping Hannah's hands between her own. "You have a huge support system in place. Everybody loved Lauren and the girls. Donations are already coming in. And your father and I will help you in whatever way we can."

Hannah cringed. She hated feeling like a charity case, but as much as it pained her to admit it, she needed the charity. When Lauren had discovered she was pregnant, Hannah promised she'd help raise the babies. Lauren's parents had died years earlier and she'd had no one.

"This house isn't ready for children," Hannah said. Her father and brother had begun working on the turn-of-the-century farmhouse as soon as Hannah and her mother had left for Boston. She wasn't complaining, but the expenses had already gotten out of hand, charity or not. The ranch was supposed to be a long-term endeavor, and now she had to rush to finish the projects she'd started after Lauren moved out. "None of this feels real. I keep waiting for her to call or pop in and yell *surprise* any minute."

Hannah pushed the sandwich away. She had the annual Christmas Dash-4-Cash barrel race on Saturday and she needed to take home first prize. She couldn't even begin to think how she'd maintain her rodeo schedule next year with the twins in tow. But giving it up was out of the question if she expected to keep a roof over their heads.

She had already spread herself too thin. Between her part-time job teaching at the rodeo school and training barrel race horses on her ranch, she hardly found time to practice her own sport. As much as she loved racing, she didn't want to be doing it when she was fifty.

She had a strong five-year plan. At least she'd thought so a week ago. She'd bought the ranch with organic farming in mind, but the large stables and round pen areas had given her the opportunity to board horses in addition to training them. Every waking hour of her day had been chock-full before the twins had become her full-time responsibility. None of her careful planning mattered anymore. Her first priority had to be Charlotte and Cheyenne, and she didn't even know where to begin.

IT WAS ALMOST ten o'clock in the evening when Noah rolled down Main Street. Ramblewood was located in the heart of Hill Country, almost two hundred miles southwest of College Station. The town was quiet except for a local honky-tonk. He wasn't sure what he'd expected to see when he drove into town. He'd had an inexplicable need to get to Ramblewood, uncertain of what he'd find or even wanted to find. He'd asked himself the same question repeatedly during the three-and-a-half-hour drive. *What will I do if the girls are mine?* Somewhere south of Austin he'd concluded he wasn't ready to be a dad. It might be a little too late for that, though.

He had passed a hotel on the way into town and decided to double back and check in for the night. After he spoke to his boss and let him know he wouldn't be coming into work until sometime after Thanksgiving, he phoned his mother. Her disappointment that he wouldn't be home for the holiday coupled with her curiosity about the business that would keep him away left him antsier than before. He loved his mom, but he felt the need to leave out the majority of the details. She'd be on the next plane to Texas complicating matters further if she knew the whole story. Once he had the paternity results, then he would tell her—if there was anything to tell.

He walked down the hotel hallway to grab a soda from the vending machine. How do you let your mom know you're the father of almost-two-year-old twins? Hell, he couldn't even fathom the fact he may have created another life, let alone two lives. His knees buckled.

He reached out for the wall to steady himself, almost knocking a fire extinguisher to the floor.

I can't breathe.

Noah barreled through the exit leading to the outdoor pool. He collapsed into one of the lounge chairs and closed his eyes, praying the world would stop spinning. Paternity test. He'd heard about them on *The Jerry Springer Show*, but he'd never actually known someone who needed to take one. He had no idea how long a test would even take, but he'd schedule it right after he found out where the girls lived. If he could find them. He had to find them. But then what? Take them home? He supposed the sooner the children had an established routine, the better. The thought alone surprised him. Hours ago, he was a childless man sitting in a bar. Now he might be the father of two, worrying about their routine. No, he definitely wasn't ready for this.

Noah had hoped to find fresh perspective by morning, but that would've required sleep. Instead, he was back in town before the sun was even above the horizon. Memorial Garden Cemetery had been simple enough to locate. The freshly covered grave and flower arrangements were visible from the street. His feet felt leaden as he forced himself out of the car and onto the lawn. The gentle autumn breeze carried the delicate scent of roses and carnations, almost teasing him with the promise of something happy.

A hand-printed sign had been placed at the head of the grave. The *L* and *E* in her name stood out long before he got close enough to read the rest. He'd been to more than his share of funerals, but he'd never seen this many flowers. The obituary had even requested donations be made to an educational fund for the girls in lieu of flowers. The phrasing had left a bad taste in his mouth. His children shouldn't need donations when he could provide for them. And he would have if he had known they existed. He snorted quietly. Here he was getting annoyed about other people providing for two kids he didn't even know were his. The sound of a truck backfiring startled him. A battered Ford pickup trundled into the cemetery on what appeared to be its last legs. *Appropriate place for it to die.* He caught a glimpse of the driver. She looked remarkably like the woman he'd pulled up on the internet last night. Hannah Tanner…one of the country's top barrel racers. Hers was the only other name mentioned in the obituary. His only lead to the truth.

He casually walked away from the grave, slipping his sunglasses on to hide his obvious perusal. After exiting the driver-side door, she lifted two tiny tots out of the passenger side. Since when was it okay for kids to ride in the front seat of a truck? Holding each of their hands in hers, they made their way slowly toward the mountain of flowers. Hannah's long copper-red hair shone in the morning sun. And that was when it hit him.

Hannah was the woman who had been with Lauren when they'd met. In the pictures he'd seen online, her hair had been pulled away from her face and she'd worn a cowboy hat. This morning she wore an unadorned black button-down dress and a cropped denim jacket along with a pair of worn cowboy boots.

He climbed back into his car as he watched them,

almost feeling guilty for intruding on their private moment. A part of him wanted to walk up and say hello. But if she recognized him, how would she explain who he was to the kids? He had been a one-night stand, nothing more. He wasn't exactly a friend, either. If only the twins would turn around and look his way. A photo in a newspaper wasn't the same as seeing them in person. He needed to be sure before he approached them.

After watching them for a few minutes, he detected the twins' subtle differences. One was slightly taller than the other. Their barely shoulder-length, rich mahogany-brown hair reminded him of Lauren's. When the shorter of the two faced his direction, he noticed hers was a shade or two lighter. Her gaze met his and he knew. His heart began to race. The urge to run to her and scoop her into his arms caught him off guard. She had his eyes—electric blue. They were piercingly visible even from a distance and he'd bet any amount of money in the world they were rimmed in black. He should go to her—to them—but his body remained frozen. Perspiration trickled down his left temple.

Before he could muster the will to approach them, they climbed into the old pickup and left. Noah's palms began to sweat against the steering wheel, which he'd been using for support. Panic set in. What if he never saw them again? Fear and anxiety gripped his heart. He may not be ready to be a father, but he couldn't walk away. Not without making absolutely sure.

He started his rental car, preparing to follow them. As they drove onto Main Street, he almost lost them at a traffic light. Once it changed, he managed to catch up while maintaining a reasonable distance until they turned onto a dusty ranch road. Quickly jotting down where he was and how he got there, he reluctantly headed into town. He could have followed them home, but that seemed creepy. He didn't want to scare them or cause Hannah to feel unsafe. Approaching them required some thought and definitely more finesse than he had at the moment.

If he planned to stay in Texas for more than one night, he needed to buy some clothes and toiletries. His original trip to Texas hadn't involved staying longer than a day. Maybe he'd be able to learn more about Hannah and her connection to the kids before he made his next move. He'd start with calling the hospital about a paternity test. If he was right, he had some enormous decisions to make. That both terrified and excited him. None of his relationships had reached the kid-talk stage. He'd assumed he would have kids someday, but he had never given much thought as to when.

Noah took a deep breath. Most men had nine months to plan for this; he hadn't even had twenty-four hours. It didn't matter. He'd love them more than life itself. Noah smiled. He already did.

THE RAP AGAINST the screen door caught Hannah by surprise. Everyone she knew didn't bother with formalities and always let themselves in.

"It's open," Hannah called from beside the living room hearth. She wanted to finish replacing the loose tiles before her mother dropped off the kids. The person knocked again.

What in the world? Hannah huffed.

She scraped off her trowel and loosely covered the tub of adhesive grout. Her parents had taken the twins over to their house to play, giving her a chance to make some repairs without them underfoot. Just when she completed one task, she'd notice another potential hazard. She'd even considered sending them to her parents' house to stay for a week or two, but she didn't want to confuse them even further. "I said it was open."

Hannah rounded the corner to the front door, surprised to see a stranger in a pantsuit peering at her through the screen.

"Miss Hannah Tanner?" the woman asked.

Hannah hesitated. The woman looked official…too official. "May I help you?"

"Are you Hannah Tanner?" the woman asked a bit more sternly.

Hannah stiffened her spine and gripped the doorframe. "I am, and who might you be?"

"I'm Constance Malone from Luna County Social Services." The woman's face showed zero expression. "I'm sorry for the loss of your friend Lauren Elgrove. Normally I would have called first, but I was unable to find a number for you. I'm here to follow up on the placement of Charlotte and Cheyenne Elgrove. May I come in?"

"I don't have a house phone, just a cell." Hannah opened the screen door, allowing her to enter. "I'm sorry, but I wasn't expecting you. I gave all my information to Social Services in Boston. I didn't realize there was anything more for me to do."

Constance glanced around the foyer toward the living room, and then in the opposite direction at the dining area, which had become a construction catchall over the past few days.

"Please pardon the mess." Hannah wrung her hands. "We're in the middle of making some improvements on the house."

"We?" Constance removed a pen and notebook from her oversized tote and began writing.

"My family and I." Hannah didn't appreciate being on the defensive in her own home. "I am trying to baby-proof the house. The girls' arrival was quite unexpected."

"Where are the children? I would like to meet them."

"They're visiting with my parents for a few hours while I work on the house." Hannah pulled her phone from her pocket. "I can call and have my mom bring them back."

"I can meet them another time." Constance stepped farther into the living room. "I understand they have lived with you before. Do you mind if I have a look around? I'm required to perform a home evaluation."

Oh, crap! "Um, sure. I wasn't exactly prepared for your visit."

"I understand this is rather sudden. Everyone involved needs time to adjust. That's why I'm here—to aid in the girls' adjustment." Constance examined the thermostat. "Do you always keep it this cold in here?" She jotted down something on her notepad.

Hannah tugged the bandanna from the top of her

head in a vain attempt to look more presentable. "I lowered it because my brother sanded the banister earlier and I wanted to air the residual dust out of the house before I damp mopped the floors. That's also why the front door was open." She ran her hand down the front of her paint-stained T-shirt.

She followed closely behind Constance for almost an hour as the woman took numerous notes. Hannah's jaw began to ache from clenching it so tightly. After a mini interrogation about her lifestyle and finances, the social worker handed her a mile-long list of items that needed to be resolved before next week's inspection.

"What happens if I can't get these completed by then?" Hannah asked. They'd been mired in long-term renovations even before they realized they'd need to baby-proof.

"Miss Tanner, we understand this is a very difficult time for you and the children." Constance removed her glasses. "It's not my intention to appear hardhearted, but your home isn't exactly a child-friendly environment. I know you were in the middle of renovations when the twins arrived, but it's my job to put their safety first. I sympathize with you, but I'm afraid if the repairs aren't made, I'll be forced to remove the children and place them in temporary foster care until your home is ready. And I'm emphasizing *temporary*. It wouldn't be forever. Just until you are better equipped to manage them."

"Foster care?" Hannah tucked her hair behind her ears. "I'm their legal guardian. Our attorneys drew up the documents when Lauren created her will before the twins were born."

"Hopefully it won't come to that." Constance gathered the paperwork she'd spread across the kitchen table. "Since you already have a couple of completed rooms and what appears to be a strong support system, I feel comfortable leaving them here with you, for now. But I urge you to complete that list. I will work with you in whatever way I can. It's clear to me you're making a valiant effort. Please be sure the children are available next week. I will be out to see you next Friday."

Hannah followed Constance to the door. Even with her family's help, it would be impossible to finish everything. "What if I move into my parents' house with the girls until the repairs are completed? Will that give me more time?"

Constance shook her head. "I'm allowing an additional two days because of Thanksgiving. I probably won't have a chance to perform another home evaluation before next Friday at a residence you may or may not be living in. You have nine days." Constance reached into her tote and removed her notepad once again. "Give me your parents' address and I'll try my best to visit them before the end of next week. No guarantees, though. So please complete that list. I try to do everything I can to prevent placing a child—let alone two—in temporary foster care before a weekend, because it ties everyone's hands until the following Monday. Thank you for your time today." She gave Hannah's hand a gentle squeeze. "I have faith you can do this, Miss Tanner."

Hannah's world tilted on its axis. She closed the front door behind Constance and scrambled into the kitchen, pushing the containers of food aside on the counter in an attempt to find her phone. *Help!* She needed it and fast. She refused to let Lauren down. Hell would freeze over before anyone took those children away from her, even temporarily.

Chapter Two

Noah had spent the majority of his afternoon getting to know Ramblewood while attempting to plan his next move. The town wasn't much different from his hometown of Aurora, Oregon. It was quaint and tidy. The kind of small town where everyone knew everyone else and children grew up, married and had children of their own. He still hadn't decided what he would do if Cheyenne and Charlotte were his children. Take them back to Aurora and raise them? Or allow them to stay in Ramblewood with Hannah, if she was their guardian? He didn't know for certain.

Being a helicopter-logging pilot made him a very methodical man, so he began with what he already knew. He steadied his nerves and drove to the ranch turnoff Hannah had taken that morning. As he approached the entrance, he stepped on the accelerator, speeding past it. Why was he so nervous? If he was correct, he had a legal right to his children. At least he thought he did.

He checked the rearview mirror and slowed down to make a U-turn so he could head back toward Hannah's...

if she even lived down that road. She could have been visiting someone. It could lead to another road, too.

As soon as he drove off the blacktop, clouds of dust engulfed the car. Within seconds, he spotted her truck in the front yard. Relief eased the tension from his neck and shoulders only to be replaced with a bout of nerves bigger than the state of Texas. He pulled in behind the pickup, stepped from the car and looked up at the two-story white clapboard farmhouse.

Noah assumed the home had been beautiful in its day. Now large sheets of paint were peeling from the siding as if trying to escape. The bare wood rail running the entire length of the expansive front porch along with the recently stripped and sanded floorboards told him it was a work in progress. Despite the repair, the house needed serious help.

The front screen door swung wide and Hannah appeared. Her coppery waves were twisted into a casual bun. Paint had splattered her faded jeans and gray T-shirt. "Can I help you?"

"I hope so." Noah jammed his hands in his pockets.

Hannah walked to the top of the stairs, shielding the sun from her eyes. "Oh, my God. It's you."

Noah didn't know if he should be thankful or scared that she recognized him. He opened his mouth to respond when two tiny faces appeared in the front door. Leaning to the right, he attempted to look past Hannah. She quickly glanced over her shoulder and shooed the girls inside.

"I thought you two were asleep on the sunporch." The screen door bounced against the door frame behind her.

"I need to talk to this man for a minute and it's your naptime. You had a busy morning at Nanny's. When you wake up, we'll play." Hannah disappeared, leaving Noah to wonder who Nanny was. It was his understanding he was the twins' only living relative.

Hannah reappeared a few minutes later. "I didn't want them to hear our conversation. They should sleep for a good hour or two." She eased the door open cautiously. "How did you find us?"

"I was in College Station and saw Lauren's obituary." Noah stood at the bottom of the porch stairs, gazing up at her. "I'm truly sorry for your loss."

"Thank you." She nibbled nervously on her bottom lip. "She tried to find you."

"I think that answers my next question." Noah swallowed hard. He gripped the car keys so tight they dug into his palm. "Am I their—"

Hannah stepped outside but remained within listening distance of the doorway. "Yes, you are."

And there it was. The answer had come much easier and faster than he'd imagined and he didn't know what to do with the information.

"I'm their father." The full impact of the words hit him once he said them aloud. He thought his legs would give out. He turned and sat on the steps, attempting to maintain steady breaths.

Hannah sat down beside him. "I can't even begin to imagine what you're feeling, but the girls have been through a lot. I will answer any questions you have, but I'm begging you, don't push this issue with them right now. Give them a chance to get to know you before announcing who you are."

Noah shifted on the stairs to face her. "Can I see them?"

Hannah nodded. Her eyes were glassy, but she didn't shed a tear. "Lauren would have loved to have seen this day." She rose and motioned for him to follow her inside. "I'm sure this is a surprise, but if it's any consolation, she did try to find you."

"I wish she hadn't run out on me the way she did. I would have liked to have gotten to know her better." As set as he was in bachelor life, there had been something special about Lauren. He'd been disappointed she hadn't left behind a phone number. And he'd searched the room, too, probably harder than he should have after such a brief encounter. At first, he thought a scrap of paper could have fallen off the dresser or the table, then possibly behind the bed. He'd searched until checkout time, and then he had no choice but to leave Lauren and their night together behind.

"She was embarrassed." Her hand lightly rested on his forearm. "Instantly falling in bed with someone wasn't Lauren's style. She was the 'sweet tea on the front porch, date a few times before a first kiss' kind of girl. Then you happened. Her life was just beginning and she didn't want anything serious. She regretted her decision."

Noah appreciated Hannah's honesty. Inside the house, he followed her through rooms in various stages of disrepair. "Pardon the mess. I'm in the middle of renovating."

He appreciated a work in progress, but practically every area was under construction. And he wasn't sure how that made him feel. Were his daughters safe here? The baby gates gave him some sense of security, but this uneasiness was unfamiliar to him. When they reached the sunroom on the back of the house, Hannah blocked his way forward.

"I'm sure you're anxious to get to know them, but I'm serious when I say I don't want them to know who you are yet." She kept her voice low. "They're still looking for Lauren. They know she's gone, but they also know she's in town and keep asking to see her at the cemetery. I've tried to explain it to them. So has my mom and Abby—she's my sister-in-law. The social worker in Boston explained it will take a while for them to adjust."

Noah adored the way Hannah protected his children. *His children.* That was going to take some getting used to.

Hannah stared up at him, as if trying to read his mind. He was all too aware of their physical closeness. At six foot three, he stood a solid eight inches taller, if not slightly more. Her crystal-blue eyes were the clearest he'd ever seen of any eye color.

She was pretty, even with messy hair and paint-splattered clothes.

She inhaled deeply, sadness replacing her curious expression. She climbed over the baby gate into the large sunroom. It was spotless, freshly painted sunny yellow. Crisp white curtains framed the windows that overlooked a long row of horse stables and a riding area.

There were four horses in one corral and two miniatures in another. In the distance, he saw more horses and dark soil-covered fields. He hadn't realized her property was this extensive. It was deceiving from the front.

Noah zeroed in on the two sleeping figures curled up together on the white, slip-covered sofa at the far end of the room. He hadn't anticipated that it would physically hurt to see them. There were two little lives less than fifteen feet away that he had helped create. Hannah reached out to wake them.

"Don't." His whisper cracked in the silence. "Let them sleep. I need to process this."

"There's a lot of that going around." A bittersweet smile graced her lips. "Would you like to sit down?" She gestured to a pair of oversized beanbag chairs on the carpeted floor. "This is their playroom."

Noah sank into a chair, letting it envelop him. He chuckled, unable to remember when he'd last sat in something so ridiculously comfortable and fun. They remained silent for a few minutes, watching the twins sleep. His nerves began to fade as the girls' rhythmic breathing relaxed him. He may have known Lauren for only one night, but her face had been ingrained in his memory. Where the girls had his eyes, they had her dark hair and rounded nose. All children were beautiful, but Noah felt as if his were extra special.

"I know they look identical, but they're fraternal twins," Hannah said. "Cheyenne is an inch taller than Charlotte. And Charlotte has a tiny birthmark under her left eye."

One of the girls stirred and sat upright before he had

a chance to ask any of the millions of questions swirling through his brain. As Hannah rose, the little girl climbed off the sofa and toddled to them. "Charlotte, this is a friend of your mommy's. His name is Noah and he came to meet you."

Charlotte's sleepy eyes blinked at him, still waking up from her nap. He had been right. Their irises were rimmed in black, the same as his were. "Go see Mommy?"

Hannah sucked her lips inward and looked toward the ceiling before answering. "Maybe tomorrow. You've already been twice today."

Charlotte reached for Noah's outstretched leg and pulled herself onto his lap. He held his breath. This little person was *his child*. His child was touching him. He stared down at her. She had little bits and pieces of him floating around inside her. It was a miracle—she was a miracle. And he couldn't wrap his head around it.

"It's okay to breathe, you know." Hannah smiled warmly at the two of them.

He wanted to hug her for welcoming him into her home and allowing him to be there. He wanted to hug his daughter, but he didn't know what was appropriate and what wasn't. It felt surreal and natural at the same time.

"So this is what twenty-one months feels like." Charlotte played with the silver cross around his neck. "They're smaller than I th—" Noah shook his head. "I don't know how big I thought they would be. I'm still overwhelmed by this. I can't even begin to imagine what they were like when they were born. I don't even know when that was."

"Valentine's Day. Which couldn't have been more appropriate considering Lauren called them the greatest loves of her life." A faraway look overshadowed Hannah's smile. "They were good-sized babies for twins. I was in the delivery room when they were born. Charlotte was 7 lbs. 2 oz. and Cheyenne was 7 lbs. 6 oz. Between my parents and me, we have a ton of pictures." She began to speak, then cut herself short. Tears filled her eyes. "Um, my mom and I weren't able to take much from her house in Boston when we picked up the girls the other day. The company she worked for has someone packing her belongings and sending them to me. When they arrive, I'd be happy to share them with you. I think it's important the children keep her memory alive, although at this age, how much can they possibly remember? Excuse me."

Hannah stood and climbed over the baby gate, disappearing down the hall. Tiny fingers touched the side of his face, rubbing the rough stubble. She giggled loudly, waking Cheyenne on the other side of the room. When Hannah reappeared, two pint-size angels were playfully attacking him with their stuffed animals.

"I apologize." She rejoined them in the sunroom. "Lauren's dea— Her not being around any longer still doesn't seem real."

"Neither does this." Noah smiled down at his daughters happily playing on his chest. "Did you and Lauren grow up together?"

"Play gently, Cheyenne," Hannah said to the bouncing toddler. "We met in college and became best friends. Lauren didn't have any family, so she came home with me on weekends, holidays and summer break. My parents thought of her as one of their own, so even though I was only a part of her life for six and a half years, she felt like a sister." She scooted closer to the girls on the floor. "The twins strengthened the bond with my family even further. They call my parents Nanny and Grandpop."

Now Noah understood who Nanny was. "When did Lauren move to Boston?"

"September." Hannah stared into the distance. "Her leaving was hard…for all of us. My mom watched the girls during the day while Lauren went to work. Let me tell you—" she smiled, visibly fighting back tears "—my mom loved every second of it. These two have her—heck, all of us—wrapped around their fingers. But then it happened." She sighed as the joy she'd expressed only a moment before slid from her face. "A pharmaceutical company in Boston offered Lauren a research scientist position. She was a biochemist—I don't know if you knew that or not. Anyway, the job had incredible medical benefits, plus on-site day care and a relocation allowance. She would have been foolish to turn it down. Their new life had so much promise and it was hard to do anything other than wish them well."

"How did it—" Noah didn't want to say the words in front of the girls.

"How did it happen?" Hannah's brows rose. "She hit a patch of ice on the way home from work. It was no one's fault. Just a cruel twist of fate."

Noah felt the need to comfort her in some way but didn't know how. *I'm sorry* didn't seem like enough.

"In case you don't have plans for tomorrow…" Hannah hesitated. "You're welcome to join us for Thanksgiving at my parents' house. It's loud and crowded, but it's a lot of fun and there will be many people sharing stories about Lauren."

Thanksgiving had always been him, a couple of the guys and football. He'd been raised by an incredible single mom. She spent her holidays serving food to the homeless in a Portland soup kitchen but had always found time to make a special Thanksgiving breakfast for just the two of them. She never included whomever she was dating at the time. Not that any of them had paid him much attention anyway. And he never knew his dad or his dad's side of the family. It was their special tradition and this was the first year he'd miss it. "I'd love to. Thank you."

He looked down at his daughters. Hovering multimillion-dollar helicopters above the tree line with two-hundred-foot logs swinging from a cable beneath him had always given him an adrenaline rush, but it was nothing compared to this.

HANNAH WAS NERVOUS Thanksgiving morning, which was ridiculous because she had no business being nervous about sitting down to a family dinner with the father of her best friend's children. While she had to admit he was attractive—if you were into the tall, sandy-blond, mouthwatering Chris Hemsworth type—she didn't have time to fawn over him. Or any man, for that matter. The clock was counting down to her next home inspection.

Hannah closed the door on the grain room in the stables. After feeding and turning out her own four horses and the thirteen boarders, she still had to muck the stalls and collect the eggs from the henhouse.

While everyone else slept off their food coma tonight, she'd be working on her house. And she still needed to find time to exercise her horse Restless for their barrel racing competition on Saturday. The prize money would about cover the cost of the raw materials necessary to pass inspection.

Ironically, the house probably would have passed a couple of months ago. It had needed some serious TLC, but she hadn't begun pulling everything apart until after Lauren left. She'd had the luxury of time on her side, or so she'd thought. She had started one project after another before completing any of them. Truth be told, she had felt a bit unsettled without Lauren and the girls around. Her concentration outside of the rodeo arena had been next to zero and having a multitude of unfinished home repairs hadn't mattered as much as they did now. She knew she'd eventually get to them. Now she didn't have a choice.

Her brother had been able to round up some friends willing to help her meet the social worker's deadline. She'd have to figure out a way to repay them afterward. Generosity was one thing, but she refused to take advantage of everyone's kindness.

For a small ranch, chores took up the majority of the day. By the time she finished, she had just enough time for a quick shower before leaving for her parents' house. She climbed the back stairs and hesitated at the door.

For a split second, she swore she saw Lauren through the window, sitting at the kitchen table feeding the girls. Her chest ached when she realized it was only Abby.

Her sister-in-law had stopped over early to help her get the girls dressed and ready the same way Hannah had helped Lauren with the girls for the first nineteen months of their lives. It had been easier then. They'd rented an apartment in the center of town after college until Hannah purchased the small ranch in April. Lauren and the girls had moved in until they'd headed to Massachusetts two months ago. She wondered how Lauren had managed in Boston by herself. She had never complained, saying each day was a blessing. She had seen the beauty and grace in the simplest of things, whereas Hannah had always questioned everything.

Thanksgiving was a casual affair at the Tanner household. She threw on a pair of jeans, an ivory draped top and her favorite pair of Old Gringo boots, which Lauren had given her last Christmas. She quickly applied a little mascara and a slick of gloss over her lips on the way out the door.

She'd given Noah the address of her parents' ranch. Back in their heyday, her parents had been sheep wool farmers. She asked him to meet them there around noon, and as she unfastened the twins' car seat buckles, he drove toward her along the main ranch road. "Let me help you," Noah said as he stepped from his car.

His arm brushed against hers as he reached into the cab and lifted Cheyenne out of her seat. Hannah shook off the tingling sensation it created, reminding herself of the Girlfriend's Golden Rule—never lust after or date your best friend's ex. Hannah gasped. The unexpected thought sucked the breath from her lungs. Any *tingle* from Noah would be completely inappropriate. She couldn't betray Lauren. She wouldn't.

"You look nice, by the way." Noah's voice snapped her to attention.

His casual comments didn't help matters. "Thank you." Every minute she spent around Noah, she understood Lauren's attraction to him more. Granted the man would be in her life forever because of the girls, but it didn't mean it was a one-way pass to a relationship.

"Are children their age permitted to ride in the front seat of the truck?"

His question knocked her off-kilter. She didn't appreciate the insinuation she was illegally toting the kids around. "I assure you it's quite legal. If a pickup truck doesn't have an extended cab, children can ride up front if they are in an appropriate car seat or safety harness." Hannah had read the manuals. She knew the rules. She'd even had the police department install the seats. There was no doubt in her mind the children were safe. Her truck wasn't ideal, but she couldn't afford a more child-friendly vehicle right now.

"Whoa, I didn't mean to offend you." Noah hip-checked the truck door closed once the twins were out. "Although I can see why you would be. I'm sorry. I guess I'm being overly protective. I mean, that's what I'm supposed to do, right? That's a fatherly thing."

Hannah tried not to laugh at his explanation. He really was new to this. "I'm the one who should apologize. You're asking the right questions. I'd be worried if you weren't. This is old hat to us Charlotte and Cheyenne veterans." She tugged at the bottom of Charlotte's dress where it had caught in her white stockings. Not that those would last more than an hour the way the kids played. "For the record, I haven't told anyone who you are yet. I mentioned I was bringing someone to dinner and figured we could tell them together. But again I ask you, please be careful what you say in front of the twins."

Noah leaned closer to Hannah so the girls wouldn't overhear. "I'm their father. You do plan on allowing me to tell them sometime soon, don't you?"

"Yes, of course." Hannah had the sinking feeling the next sixteen and a half years would be much harder than she'd imagined. He'd probably ask for a visitation schedule. She wasn't ready for any overnight visits to his house and neither were the girls. "I've spent almost every day of their lives with them. I know what's best. Trust me."

Hannah introduced Noah to all sixteen members of her family—newly enlarged courtesy of her brother Clay's marriage to Abby.

Once the girls were playing safely out of earshot, Hannah gathered her parents, brother and sister-in law together in the kitchen.

"I have something to tell you," Hannah began. Her stomach clenched. "Noah isn't just a friend of mine. He's Charlotte and Cheyenne's biological father."

"Heaven help us." Hannah's mother reached for the counter to steady herself. "What does this mean?"

"It doesn't mean anything yet." Hannah spoke before

Noah had a chance to respond. "The girls don't know and we need to take this day by day."

Noah excused himself, and for a brief second, Hannah wondered if he was making a break for it. From the outside looking in, she could see how her clan could be a tad intimidating.

"Why didn't you call me as soon as Noah made contact with you?" Clay demanded. "I need to run him through the system and make sure he's legit. I assume you're going to schedule a paternity test. Taking this man at his word isn't smart or safe."

Hannah reeled from her brother's onslaught of questions and demands. It was the downside to having a private investigator in the family. "I'm quite certain he'll want a paternity test. But I'm positive he's the father. He was the only person Lauren had been with during that time. As for a background check, I'm fine with it. I don't think he needs to know, though."

"Where does he even live?" Clay asked. "And what are his intentions with the twins?"

"I don't know." Lauren and Noah hadn't spent much of their night together talking. And Hannah hadn't thought to ask during his visit yesterday afternoon. "He met Lauren in College Station and he learned of her death there, too, so I'm assuming he lives somewhere in that vicinity." It wasn't next door, but three and a half hours away would allow him to visit on weekends. Maybe after a while she'd even be willing to make up a guest room for him so he could spend more time with his daughters.

Clay rolled his eyes. "My naive little sister, things

aren't always as they appear on the surface. What's his last name? I'll have one of my associates begin working on it."

Hannah hadn't remembered him mentioning a last name. She groaned inwardly. "I have no idea. I took him at his word." Maybe she had more of Lauren in her than she thought.

"I'll handle it. Until we know more about him, you should limit his time with the twins and make sure someone else is there when he's around." Clay enveloped her in a hug.

"I know this is hard, kiddo." Hannah's father joined them. "We'll help you through it any way we can. Clay's right, though. Until we know more about him, you need to keep your distance. At the very least, have one of us there with you."

They rejoined the rest of the family as Noah reappeared bearing a bouquet for her mother and a couple of bottles of wine for her father. Her parents appreciated the sweet gesture. Something Lauren used to say came to mind: "You can't fake sincerity." Hannah had always argued that fact, until yesterday. Noah seemed genuinely enamored with his daughters, which was what Lauren had always hoped for. She had always vowed to find him one day.

By the end of dinner, Clay had grilled Noah more than a steak on a barbecue. His last name was Knight… as in shining armor. Lauren would have howled at that. And his first name was William. But there had been so many Williams in his kindergarten class he'd asked the teacher to use his middle name instead. He went by

Noah from then on. That explained why Clay hadn't been able to locate a pilot named Noah when Lauren asked him to find the father of her unborn babies. His job as a helicopter-logging pilot sounded as cool as it did dangerous.

"Aren't you concerned with deforestation?" Hannah's father, Gage, asked.

"Heli-logging actually works in harmony with the environment. Instead of scarring the hillside by dragging the logs out or building new roads to transport them, I'm able to lift a telephone pole–sized log straight up."

"So you're not creating huge sections of missing trees?" Abby asked.

"No, we're not clear-cutting," Noah continued. "We're also eliminating the soil erosion that can arise from traditional logging." Noah reached across the table for the salt and pepper shakers and placed them in front of his plate. "Heli-logging thins the forest and opens it up by creating wide spaces between the trees." He moved the shakers apart from one another to demonstrate. "You're always hearing about forest fire devastation. A fire will whip through a thinned forest and rarely burn a tree because it remains on the ground. When a forest hasn't been managed—" he moved the shakers closer together "—there are felled trees and overgrowth providing fuel that concentrates and intensifies the heat on the ground." He placed his silverware and napkin around and between the shakers. "The fire doesn't have a chance to flash through as it does in a managed forest. It's never a matter of *if* there will be a forest fire, it's when. Heli-logging helps control the burn before it begins. That's just one aspect of the job."

"I never knew any of that existed." Fern offered him more sweet potatoes. "Your life definitely sounds interesting."

Charlotte and Cheyenne had insisted on sitting next to him at the table and Hannah wondered if they instinctively knew he was their father.

What had surprised Hannah most was that he lived two thousand miles away in Oregon. She and the girls definitely wouldn't be seeing him as much as she'd anticipated. That unsettled her. A weekly visitation schedule would be better for the girls. How could they bond with him if they were together only a few times a year?

"Noah," her father said. "I don't know what your plans are for the rest of the evening, but we have a tradition of cutting down a live Christmas tree and decorating it on Thanksgiving. We'd love to have you join us, since you're the expert logger."

Noah laughed. "I'd be honored, sir. But my team does most of the cutting on the ground. I'm more of a removal man. Hopefully you don't choose a tree large enough for me to bring in one of my Chinook helicopters."

Hannah hadn't expected to enjoy decorating the tree when the men returned. She'd made up her mind earlier that she would duck out just after they left on their tree expedition. It was too painful without her best friend there. Her family's high spirits kept the mood elevated even though everyone felt Lauren's absence. The girls had fallen asleep shortly after they'd brought the boxes of decorations down from the attic. Thankfully, her mother had kept their cribs after Lauren left for Boston. They'd return to their old routine of staying with Nanny during the day once Hannah went back to work at the rodeo school. Her job had graciously given her time off while she settled the house and the girls' routine.

"These were Lauren's." Her mother carefully un-wrapped the tissue paper–covered ornaments. "I had promised to send them to her once she'd settled in. Now I will pass them directly on to her daughters."

Noah sat on the couch beside her mother and wrapped a supportive arm around her shoulders. "I'll make sure they're the first ornaments the girls hang every year, and I'll even send you pictures."

"Excuse me?" Hannah stared at Noah. "You make it sound as if Charlotte and Cheyenne will be with you."

Noah looked around the room and stood. "Where else would they be? I'm their father."

"And I'm their legal guardian." Hannah took a step toward him. "Father or not, Lauren named me in her will, not you."

"Only because she didn't know where to find me," Noah countered. "You even said she'd been looking for me."

"She may have been looking for you, but she had no intention of handing her children over to you. You have no legal claim to them."

"I will once I take a paternity test, which I've sched-uled for tomorrow at Grace General Hospital."

"You did what?" Hannah couldn't believe what was happening. He honestly expected to take the girls away from her and her family? "Who do you think you are, coming into my home, my parents' home, and announcing your plans to rip Charlotte and Cheyenne from the only family they've ever known?" Her pulse quickened and the room began to spin. He couldn't take them. She refused to consent to it. She grabbed hold of her brother's arm for support.

Clay stepped between them. "Noah, I think you should leave."

"I don't understand." Noah held up his hands. "Please don't take this the wrong way, but I've seen your house and you're clearly struggling financially. I don't want my daughters to be a burden. Plus, we have a lot of time to make up for."

"First of all, a social worker has already completed a home inspection and I'm well aware of what needs to be done to my house. And second, I may not make as much as you, but those children will never be a burden to me. We won't be millionaires, but we will survive."

"I don't want my daughters to just survive. I want them to thrive and I can provide that for them."

Hannah felt a shiver down to the bone. "A few hours ago you wondered if asking questions regarding their safety was the fatherly thing to do. You don't have experience with these children. There's no way in hell you're getting those girls."

"I understand your attachment to them." Noah spoke with controlled firmness. "I would never cut you out of their lives. That wouldn't be fair to them or you. But I am their biological father, and you can't keep me from raising them. You're more than welcome to visit anytime you'd like, but those girls are coming home with me."

Clay grabbed Noah by the collar and ushered him to the door. "Until you have a court order saying otherwise, stay away from my sister and my family." He pushed him through the door and slammed it shut behind him.

"Oh, my God." Fern began to cry. "Does he have a chance of getting the girls?"

Clay glared down at his sister. "You need to prepare yourself for the fight of your life." He gripped Hannah's shoulders. "Maybe I can uncover something to use against him in court. Call Avery. You need an attorney to help you fight this. If a paternity test proves he's their biological father, a judge can sever your claim to them, despite Lauren's will."

This must be a cruel joke. Charlotte and Cheyenne were a part of her as if they were her own flesh and blood. She'd already lost her best friend—she refused to lose the girls, too. She felt a steely grip squeeze her heart. *Lauren.* She never would have wanted this.

Chapter Three

"Thank you for seeing me so fast." Hannah pulled her jacket tighter across her chest while she waited for Avery Griffin to unlock the front door of her law offices.

Avery gave Hannah one of the coffees she'd picked up on the way in and held the door open for her to enter. "I'm glad you called me, and don't worry, I'll take your case pro bono. I know this is difficult." She adjusted the thermostat on the wall. "Have a seat."

"I'm grateful for your help. I'm worried an attorney will cause Noah to move faster. You should have heard him yesterday." Hannah sipped her coffee in an attempt to get warm. She didn't know if she shook out of nervousness or if it was because the temperature had dropped twenty degrees overnight. "I can't sit by and let him tear Charlotte and Cheyenne away from my family."

"Don't worry about upsetting Noah. I'm sure he assumes you have an attorney, since we had to handle the guardianship papers when Lauren died. And he may have already retained one, too. Let's start with the facts." Avery removed a legal pad from her top drawer and began to take notes. "Paternity hasn't been established. Until it is, Noah can't do anything. You have two choices. You can willingly submit the girls to be DNA tested, which would involve an inner mouth swab, or you can wait for a judge to issue a court order requiring testing. Personally, unless there is a valid reason to delay it, I strongly recommend complying with the request. If this case goes to court, it shows your willingness to cooperate."

Hannah's mouth went dry despite the coffee. "I didn't have a problem with the paternity test until now. I knew Lauren better than anyone, and I—" Saying her name in the past tense made swallowing difficult. She cleared her throat. "I'm sorry."

Avery handed her a tissue and joined her on Hannah's side of the desk. "It's okay. I understand."

"Lauren didn't sleep around. She hadn't been with anyone else for about a year before the twins were conceived." Hannah began to shred the tissue. "Lauren had hoped to find Noah one day, but only because she thought her children deserved to know who their father was. Despite the connection she had felt with him that night, she wasn't looking to spend the rest of her life with him. She wanted him to have a chance to coparent the children with her. I'm asking for the same courtesy."

"A judge is interested in the facts and the best interest of the children," Avery said. "You have a strong case, but it's not cut-and-dried. Before the wrong judge, his paternity might carry more weight. This type of case is best settled out of court. Both of you have too much to lose. I'd like to call Noah in for a meeting to see if we can work out some sort of mediation."

"Do you need me to be there?" She was still too angry with him. Her family had opened their home to him and he'd thanked them by threatening to take the twins away.

Avery shook her head. "I don't want Noah to think we're ganging up on him. If it's just the two of us, he might be more willing to discuss a visitation schedule."

"Visitation meaning he visits the children in my home, not the other way around," Hannah clarified. "He made a comment yesterday that led me to believe he is financially well-off."

Avery reached for her iPad and flipped the cover open. "Your brother emailed me a very detailed report on Noah this morning. Financially he's sound. His skill set earns him a higher than average income, but he's a long way from being a millionaire. Noah's also very clean. He served eight years in the air force, owns his own home, has zero police violations and is one of the world's best heli-logger pilots. He conducts seminars in the United States and around the world."

"Wouldn't that give me the advantage?" It was the first ounce of hope she'd felt all morning. "How can he be there for his children if he's traveling?"

"Don't you travel across the country barrel racing?"

"Yes, but it's different. My parents can watch the girls. I'm never gone for very long. Many times my mom comes with me, so bringing the girls along wouldn't be a problem. He said during dinner yesterday that he only has his mom, and if he travels out of the country—"

Hannah's stomach flipped. "He can't take the girls to another country, can he?"

"There's no denying you have a great support system." Avery patted Hannah's forearm. "We're getting ahead of ourselves. Are you open to some form of a temporary arrangement granting him visitation while we attempt to hash out a resolution?"

"As long as it remains civil." Hannah sighed. "I think Noah is as scared as I am about losing the girls, but for different reasons. I'm more than willing to give this another chance, if he is."

"Then let's get to work." Avery walked behind her desk. "I'll try to arrange a meeting with Noah today."

Hannah didn't want to be unreasonable. Lauren had seen something in Noah and she owed it to her friend to give him a chance.

Noah wasn't overly surprised when Hannah's attorney phoned and asked to meet with him later that afternoon. He parked his rental car in front of the law offices. He needed to steady his nerves before he went inside. He was still reeling from yesterday. He preferred to get his excitement on the job, not around a family Christmas tree. Granted, he could have handled himself better, but they could have, too. Between the barrage of questions and the obvious assumption he would be a casual father to Charlotte and Cheyenne, he'd about reached his breaking point on the way back from their Christmas tree trek in the woods. Halfway there he began to wonder if the whole cutting down a tree on Thanksgiving story hadn't been a ruse to separate him from Hannah and the twins so they could break him down.

He got it. Clay was defending Lauren's honor after Noah had gotten her pregnant. But he'd also hoped to see her again. Although he'd never been a fan of the whole long-distance thing, maybe they could have found a way to make it work. And then he wouldn't have missed out on the first twenty-one months of his children's lives.

Avery Griffin greeted him at the door. Tall, curvy and blonde, she looked more like a '50s Hollywood starlet than an attorney. She couldn't have been much over thirty, if that.

"Are you up for a walk?" Avery asked. "I know it's unconventional, but I've been cooped up in my office all day and I could use the exercise after eating too much yesterday."

"Sure." He began to relax as they cut down a side street toward Ramblewood Park. Noah would take wide-open spaces over a stifling office any day. "I have to admit, I expected a call, but I'm surprised you wanted to meet so soon."

"Under normal circumstances, we would've waited until Monday. Since you live out of state and we don't know your travel schedule, we didn't want to risk missing you."

Noah laughed. "I guess that's a nice way of telling me you're putting me on notice."

"Quite the opposite." Avery pulled a pair of sunglasses out of her pocket. "If this goes to court, everybody loses, especially Charlotte and Cheyenne. I'm going to explain to you how the process works so you're as informed as Hannah."

Noah stopped walking. "The process needs to start with a paternity test, which I've already scheduled."

"Hannah doesn't have a problem establishing paternity." Avery faced him. "She had a problem with the way you went about it. It's my understanding you didn't ask her for a paternity test. Instead, you told her you had already scheduled one. Technically she doesn't have to comply without a court order, since she is their legal guardian. But she wants this settled just as much as you do."

Noah agreed he had been a bit overzealous and could have handled the testing better. Off in the distance he watched an aerial fire truck raise its platform to the top of a light post so the firefighters could hang a large white snowflake.

"Do you realize what I have missed?" Noah began walking again. He had the urge to run the park's track a few times to burn off his frustration. "Hannah told me Lauren had walked out the following morning because she'd been embarrassed about our night together." Noah clenched his fists. "Think about that. Lauren's shame over having sex *with me* robbed me of the entire pregnancy experience. I never saw their first ultrasounds or heard their first heartbeats. I have no idea what either of my daughters' first words were or when they took their first steps. If she had actually talked to me before she left, all of this could have been avoided. I'm their father and I'm not going to miss another moment. The paternity test is only a formality."

Avery smiled. "Honestly, I wish I heard that from more men. I applaud you for taking the initiative, but there is a legal procedure you need to be aware of. Once we confirm paternity, I'll contact a caseworker. A guardian ad litem will then be assigned to the girls."

"Is that another lawyer?" Noah asked.

"A guardian ad litem is an advocate who ensures Charlotte and Cheyenne's best interests are always protected. I strongly advise you and Hannah to come to some form of a resolution before either one of your hands is forced."

Noah wouldn't mind having the opportunity to apologize to Hannah and her family for his behavior. He didn't want to create tension between them, he just wanted to be with his baby girls. "I wouldn't even know where to begin."

Avery clasped her hands together. "I know the perfect place."

HANNAH FINISHED LOADING Restless into the horse trailer before running inside to grab her purse. She gave Charlotte and Cheyenne a quick kiss goodbye in their car seats, then waved to them as her mother drove away. She had two hours before she needed to be at the Christmas Dash-4-Cash barrel race. She was never this nervous before a race, but after the week from hell, she'd barely had a chance to practice. Clay had loaned her his quad cab pickup, but she'd been too anxious to let the twins ride with her. Her family would meet her at the arena.

As she locked the front door, she heard the sound of

tires crunching against gravel. She'd expected to see anyone except Noah.

She ran down the front steps in the direction of her horse trailer. "I have a show to get to, Noah. I can't do this with you now."

"I know you do," he called out behind her. "I wanted to ride with you or…at least…follow you there." His words trailed off in an unexpected shyness.

Regardless of what she decided, she figured she'd regret her decision fifteen minutes down the road. Maybe he'd distract her enough to calm her nerves. "Come on." She motioned for him to join her. "FYI, though…the twins have already gone ahead with my mom."

"That's all right." He ran to catch up with her. "It will give us a chance to talk."

Hannah slid behind the wheel. "Can you behave?" she asked through the open passenger window. "This is a big race for me and, as you so graciously pointed out the other day, I need the money."

"About that." Noah climbed in and fastened his seat belt. "I was completely out of line."

"Who told you I was racing today? Not that it was a secret, but I'm surprised you know—it was Avery, wasn't it?"

He nodded. Hannah eased the truck onto the main road. Avery had wanted them to talk… Now they had the time. Alone. Away from prying eyes and prying ears. Suddenly the interior of her brother's truck seemed extremely small. She became acutely aware of every breath Noah took. Every movement involving the left side of his body sent an electric twinge pulsating through her veins.

Oh! This can't be happening.

"Why barrel racing?"

His question broke her thoughts. "Believe it or not, my mom used to be a champion barrel racer. I guess you could say it's in my blood. What little girl doesn't want to be like her mother when she's growing up? Mom became my instructor and I fell in love with the sport and the lifestyle. The rodeo isn't just about competing. It's about family, too. Besides, I was always on a horse helping my dad round up our sheep." Hannah glanced over at Noah, surprised to see him listening intently. "I told you the other day they used to raise sheep for wool. It had been lucrative until the economy took a dive and he was forced to sell their herd and the majority of their land. They married young—like seventeen young. I can't even imagine getting married at twenty-four, let alone— Never mind. Long story short, he raised sheep and she raced horses. I don't just compete, though. I also teach at the local rodeo school and I'm turning part of my land into an organic farm. Barrel racers don't ride forever."

"Okay, I get that organic farming is the rage right now, but it seems like an odd choice for a rodeo girl."

"Not really. A good portion of competitors are raised on farms. One in seven working Texans is in some form of agriculture, which isn't too surprising when you consider we have almost 250,000 farms in the state. Granted, my decision was a little more personal. Growing up, the doctors thought I had food allergies. My parents constantly had to rush me to the hospital because of something I had eaten. After countless tests, it was determined I was having reactions to the pesticides used on most of our food. So I studied agricultural science in college. I eat organic because I have to, but my goal is to educate others on the danger of pesticides and genetically modified foods. It takes three years and a lot of preparation before land can be classified as USDA certified organic. I'm in the fertilization stage, but I'll get there. It takes time and dedication."

"That's commendable." She glanced over at him and found him studying her. "You said you wanted to educate people. Do you mean teaching at a school?"

"More like a community garden for the grade school kids." Hannah had more ideas for her land than she had acreage. "I'm planning high rotation crops, which means they'll mature in sixty days or less. I'd like to give the school an acre or two so their students can gain hands-on experience with organic farming. Providing someone doesn't get certified before me, I'll be the first USDA certified organic farm in Ramblewood."

"And you can do all of that and barrel race?"

"Not exactly. Once my farm is fully operational, then I'll retire from racing and possibly teaching at the rodeo school. I'll continue to train horses to barrel race, though. Right now, I spend the majority of my time practicing for my own races and training many of the horses I board. At least that's what I was doing until the twins moved back in. My mom is super supportive and always around to help out."

"What's it like when you're competing?" Noah asked. "It seems like a lot of work for such a short race."

People had asked Hannah almost every question under the sun, but she couldn't recall anyone ever asking her that one. "It's my version of flying, only at a slower pace of forty miles an hour. Depending on the size of the arena, it's about thirteen to fifteen seconds of freedom with my horse. We both place our absolute trust in one another to make the right decisions and follow them through. I guess you could call it a marriage of sorts, only there's no spouse talking back to you."

When Noah didn't respond, she stole another glance in his direction. He was leaning partially against the door, smiling at her.

"Say something. I'm nervous enough about today's race—don't make it worse."

"I sincerely hope I don't make you nervous." His voice sounded deeper and richer than it had moments before.

"Considering the situation we're in, I'd have to say yes, you definitely do." He made her nervous for other reasons she refused to admit. She felt guilty enough for feeling the slightest attraction to Noah Knight. Of all the men in the world, he was definitely the most off-limits.

"I haven't followed a lot of barrel racing, but I've seen it on television. The way they make the turns around the barrels, it almost looks as if the horse is about to topple over on the rider. It has to be dangerous."

"It's not the safest sport, but it's a lot safer than heli-logging. Have you thought about that at all? I'm not trying to start a fight with you, but the other day you told my dad you have one of the most dangerous jobs in the world, and I'd be remiss if I didn't question how suitable a job it is for a single parent. They've already lost their mother. How fair would it be if they lost you, too?"

The cab instantly filled with tension. She would've been better off keeping her mouth shut until they both had a place to escape to.

"There are plenty of single parents with dangerous careers and the courts don't take their children away." Noah's even tone surprised Hannah. She'd offended him and he was doing his damnedest to keep it together.

"I think you and I just came to our first mutual understanding. We're actually concerned about each other's safety—for the sake of the children."

Her attempt to lighten the mood fell flat. She kept waiting for him to ask questions about Lauren or the girls, but he didn't. If the situation had been reversed, he'd have to duct tape her mouth shut to get her to stop asking questions.

"What about you? What do you do when you're not working?"

"Fishing and hiking with the guys. Believe it or not, I like to trail ride horses, although it's been a few years. I love nature, so I try to be outside as much as possible. I live on the Willamette River, so I'm spoiled in that regard. I can't imagine living anyplace else, although I've lived and traveled all over the world."

"When you were in the air force?"

Noah's silence caused her to look in his direction. "I don't remember telling you I was in the air force. And my night with Lauren may be a little hazy, but I don't believe I told her, either."

Hannah and her big mouth. "My brother ran a background check on you." There was no sense denying it. She just wished she didn't feel like the lowest form of human life for going behind his back. Although technically it had been Clay's idea.

"I should be furious with you, but I'm not," Noah said. "I did recon on you before I ever got to town. It wasn't anywhere near as extensive as yours was, but I understand the reasoning behind it. You want what's best for the girls and so do I. And yes, I traveled extensively while I was in the air force. I've been to six continents, and someday I hope to make it to Antarctica. They have some amazing cruise expedition packages. I'd love to take the girls when they're older. And you, too, if you're up for the whole glacial experience."

"You really take this outdoors thing seriously, don't you?" She laughed. "It sounds like fun."

Hannah fielded questions about the twins the rest of the way to the arena. As much as she loved Lauren, she wished her friend hadn't run out on Noah. He should have had the chance to experience the girls' lives firsthand, not through recollections.

She pulled her truck into the competitors' lot and set the parking brake. As she opened the door, Noah reached out and stilled her arm. Her pulse quickened. Hannah wanted to face him, but at the same time she was afraid to. Steeling her nerves, she closed the door and turned to him. He'd already unfastened his seat belt and was leaning over the center console. She froze when his hand rested on top of hers.

"I don't know what I'm supposed to say here." Noah's smile widened. "Is it good luck? Break a leg? Go get 'em?"

Hannah laughed. She slid her hand out from under his and hopped from the truck. "Good luck is fine," she said before closing the door.

Get a grip, girl. For a moment there, she had thought Noah was about to kiss her. She looked skyward and said a silent prayer of thanks. His presence in her life was distraction enough. She had to hand it to Lauren— her friend had chosen a man who could set a woman's belly on fire with only a wink and a smile. Too bad his charms wouldn't work on Hannah.

Chapter Four

If Noah had any thoughts of joining Hannah's family in the stands to watch her race, they vanished the moment he climbed the steps. Clay and Gage flanked either side of the row, looking none too pleased he had invited himself to the event. Rather than risk making a scene, he opted to approach them later so he could apologize for Thursday's incident.

It didn't stop him from waving to Charlotte and Cheyenne. They were dressed adorably in little reindeer outfits and antler hoodies. He wanted nothing more than to run over and pull them both into a hug, but he kept his distance. Damned if it didn't hurt like hell doing so.

Noah had been to a few hometown rodeos when he was growing up, but nothing this large. Between the parade of horses during the opening ceremony and the rodeo clown dance off, he couldn't remember the last time he had cheered so loud outside of a football game.

When the announcer said Hannah's name, every nerve in his body began to tingle in anticipation. Perched on the edge of his seat, he clasped his hands in front of him. The bell rang and Hannah's horse flew into the center of the ring, hugging the barrel to the right as they maneuvered around it before galloping toward the barrel on the left side of the dirt arena. Their movements perfectly in tune with one another, Hannah turned them and raced toward the center barrel, then sprinted to the finish line. He held his breath the entire time. And when they announced she'd set a new record, he couldn't have been more proud. Neither could Charlotte and Cheyenne. They clapped their hands wildly along with the crowd.

When it was over, Noah walked out of the event center alone. He'd waited until her family exited before he'd stood to leave. Watching someone else carry his daughters had physically pained him. They should have been sitting with him…not shielded from him.

Noah spotted Hannah outside and ran over to her.

"Congratulations!" He gave her a celebratory hug in the parking lot before his brain had a chance to register what he was doing. He released her and stepped back. The annoyance on her friends' and family's faces spoke volumes. He couldn't blame them after the argument on Thanksgiving. "I'm sorry." He cleared his throat. "I guess I got caught up in the moment there. Congratulations anyway."

If the close contact annoyed Hannah, she didn't let it show. "Thank you." She lightly touched his arm, steering him away from the makeshift entourage gathering around her outside the event center. "I know this is awkward for both of us."

Noah followed her to the truck. "It is, but I thought

we made progress earlier." Maybe he had misread their conversation on the way to the rodeo.

"We did." Hannah glanced down at the gold-and-silver belt buckle she'd won after claiming first place.

"I won't pretend to understand how the scoring works or what the 1D, 2D, 3D business is, but I'm glad you won, even though it was over so fast."

"Blink at a rodeo and you might miss something. All events happen in a matter of seconds." Hannah folded her check in half and slid it into her pocket. "*D* stands for division and I won first place in the first division. This is one of the higher-paying events of the season."

He expected her to be in a more cheerful mood after winning. She opened the truck door, chucked her cowboy hat and buckle on the seat and unbanded her hair. A quick toss of her head spilled her strawberry-hued waves forward to frame her face angelically.

"I enjoyed getting to know you better on the way here," she said as she began unsnapping the front of the Western shirt she'd worn during her ride. He could have sworn his bottom jaw smacked his chest in awe. Unaware of her effect on him, she turned away as the shirt slid down her arms, exposing her bare shoulders. Noah's body stiffened, and he willed himself not to look. Then he noticed the spaghetti-strapped white cotton camisole she wore underneath. He didn't know if he should be relieved or disappointed. She tugged a pink T-shirt from her bag and slipped it over her head before returning her attention to him. "It doesn't change anything between us. We both want to raise the girls.

I'd like to be your friend, but I think it only complicates the situation."

"Excuse me." Fern Tanner squeezed between them holding Charlotte and Cheyenne in each of her arms. "I think these two want to celebrate with you." Noah fell more in love with their reindeer outfits now that he saw them up close. That was until Fern effectively shut him out by keeping her back to him. And it was understandable. He still hadn't had a chance to apologize. He wanted to, but he didn't know quite how to go about it. His feelings were justified, but he could've handled the situation better.

"Mrs. Tanner, I owe you an apology for the other day." There. He said it, probably a little too quick to be believable. "Your family had graciously invited me into your home and I didn't mean to upset you or your husband." If anyone expected him to apologize for wanting to raise his daughters, they'd have to wait a lifetime. The inexplicable tug at his heart grew by the hour. For a man who'd never given much thought to children, he couldn't imagine walking away from these two.

Fern's entire body sagged at the sound of his voice. Charlotte attempted to reach over her shoulder to Noah, forcing Fern to face him. Fern handed Cheyenne to Hannah while attempting to reel in Charlotte's hands.

"It's okay, Mom." Hannah bounced Cheyenne on her hip. "If she wants Noah to hold her, then let him."

Fern begrudgingly allowed Noah to take Charlotte into his arms. The little girl placed her tiny hands on either side of his face and frowned.

"Fur gone." Sadness was evident in her big blue eyes.

Noah pouted and rubbed his nose against hers. "I had to shave, baby." In hopes it would give him a more fatherly appearance, he'd decided to lose the perpetual five o'clock shadow he'd maintained for a year. He might not have had such a role model growing up, but he knew how he wanted to look for his daughters.

"No!" She frowned.

"No?" *I still can't believe this bundle of cuteness is mine.* His heart felt as if it would burst at any moment. "Don't you want me to look good?"

Charlotte glanced left, then right while she pondered his question, then shrugged and rested her head, antlers and all, against his shoulder. Her body relaxed against his and he'd bet all the money in the world her eyes were heavy with sleep.

He squeezed his own shut. He wasn't a crying man, but damn if he wasn't on the verge.

"Want pacas," Cheyenne said in Hannah's arms.

"You want to see the pacas?" Hannah's animated expression triggered an instantaneous giggle fit as the toddler clapped her hands together excitely. "You'll see the pacas later when you visit Nanny." Hannah looked up at Noah. "Clay and Abby raise alpacas and my mom brings the twins over there to see them. Neither one of the girls has mastered the word yet, so we call them pacas."

Noah nodded, although he didn't know much about them. He envisioned a llama but wasn't quite sure. Didn't they spit? Between Hannah's horses and an alpaca ranch, the kids had been exposed to lots of animals. While his house was far from suburbia, outside of the occasional critter that traipsed through his property, his life was animal-free. He began to wonder how much the girls would miss once they lived with him full-time.

"Ride horsey?" Cheyenne chattered.

"Not today, sweetie. I have a lot of work to do on the house, so we won't be able to ride horses until next week."

"They ride? Aren't they a little young?" How could someone so tiny handle something that large? The thought alone terrified him. "What's next...barrel racing?"

"If they want to learn how to race, I'll teach them." Hannah raised her chin in defiance. "The majority of my students are kids. I give private lessons to a three-year-old barrel racer."

"There's a big difference between twenty-one months and three years." At least Noah thought there was. He tried to recall the children he knew and drew a blank. None of his friends had kids that young. "And it's safe?"

"I beg your pardon, Mr. Knight." Fern's hands flew to her hips, her chest puffed out like a hen ready to do battle. "I've held my tongue long enough with you."

"Mom, please." Hannah pressed Cheyenne's head to her shoulder. "Not in front of the girls."

Fern exhaled and smiled icily. "My daughter was on horses before she could walk and I never had anyone tell me I was being irresponsible." Her tone may have softened, but there was no mistaking the edge in her voice. "Lauren was also an accomplished rider and had the girls on a horse before they were a year old. She was like a daughter to me. I won't allow you to come into our lives and take away everything that was and still is Lauren."

"Mom, I can handle this." Hannah stepped in between her mom and Noah. "I respect your concerns, but I need you to respect my knowledge and trust that I'm not putting the girls in harm's way. I'm not going to stand here and defend Lauren or myself. My mom shouldn't have to, either. I don't want this to go to court, Noah." Cheyenne fussed in her arms. Hannah hugged the toddler tight and whispered in her ear. "How about some ice cream before we leave?" Charlotte's head popped up from Noah's shoulder. "You heard that, huh? I thought you were sleeping." Hannah's smile was tense. "You're welcome to join us."

"Hannah, I don't think—"

"Mom, please. We have to learn how to get along if this is ever going to work."

Noah's jaw twitched. He appreciated Hannah's efforts to keep the peace, but they didn't ease any of his concerns. But there was a time and place for this conversation and he agreed with Hannah's silent declaration… this was not it.

"I loaded Restless in the trailer." Clay wedged himself between them, stopping to lift the twins out of Noah's and Hannah's arms. "Abby and I will take the girls for ice cream, and then I'll ride home with you. Noah, I'm assuming you came here with my sister. I'll be a gentleman and find you a ride back to Ramblewood with someone."

"That's not necessary, Clay." Hannah sighed.

Noah would give her this much, she definitely had a team of supporters rallying around her. Too much so.

"Yes, it is," Clay said through clenched teeth. "There are some things we need to discuss and they can't wait."

Noah didn't need a pine tree to fall on his head to understand that *some things* meant him.

"Fine." Hannah closed the truck door and leaned against it. She waited until her brother and the rest of the family were out of earshot before she spoke. "How would you feel if I came into your world and started criticizing everything?" Her chin began to tremble. "You do realize the day will come when that will happen to you. If not by me, certainly by a social worker who will scrutinize every inch of where you live and then weigh in on your job."

Noah hadn't thought that far ahead. Avery had advised him to retain his own attorney, which he planned to do on Monday. The idea of a stranger determining his suitability as a parent frightened him. The same way his actions were frightening Hannah.

"You're right. If the situation were reversed, I'd probably feel the same way. And I'm sure I'll be just as terrified of my own home inspection." Hannah's renovations aside, her home was located in a much more kid-friendly location than the steep banks of the Willamette River that his house overlooked.

Hannah's body visibly relaxed somewhat and her face softened. "I'm willing to bet you wouldn't think twice about taking the girls up in a helicopter. I'm not talking about taking them heli-logging. I mean a helicopter joyride over the Oregon mountains. What I'm doing isn't any different. I don't want the girls to grow up scared of the world. I want them to fly in a helicopter and ride a horse at forty miles an hour…if they want to. I want them to make their own decisions and they need to experience life in order to do so."

"You don't understand. They're not a part of you."

Hannah's head snapped as if he had physically smacked her. "You may have contributed to their DNA, but that doesn't make you a father. You haven't earned that title yet. You helped create them, nothing more. I have been with Charlotte and Cheyenne almost every day of their little lives. When they went to Boston, my heart broke. I lost a piece of myself. Don't you dare tell me they're not a part of me. They're definitely more a part of me than they are of you. You just met them."

"Through no fault of my own."

Hannah crossed her arms. "Oh, really. You had a one-night stand with Lauren. If either of you had taken the time to get to know the other before jumping in bed, you would have known about your children. I blame both of you."

He couldn't argue with her logic. And she was right. Hannah was more a part of the girls than he was and he needed to acknowledge it before he lost any chance of custody.

"You're riding home with me and the twins." Fern jabbed him in the arm. "I don't want to hear any arguments about it."

"Mom!" Hannah looked around. "I thought you were with Abby and the girls."

Fern waggled her finger at Hannah. "I don't want

any arguments from you, either. Noah and I have a few things to discuss. And wipe that expression off your face. I'm not going to do anything to him." Fern turned to face him. "But we do need to come to an understanding and there's no better time than today."

After ice cream, Noah said goodbye to Hannah and hesitantly climbed into the front seat beside Fern. If Charlotte and Cheyenne weren't with them, he would have bailed. He wasn't afraid of Hannah's mother... Okay, maybe he was a little bit. It was more that he didn't want the girls to pick up on their tension. Five minutes into the drive the twins were fast asleep, leaving Noah alone to deal with Fern's wrath.

"I have two rules," she began. "Don't hurt my daughter, and don't hurt the girls." Fern held up her hand to prevent him from responding. "If you take them to Oregon, you will be hurting everyone in their lives. That's all I'm going to say on the matter...today. I want to hear more about you, your family and where you see yourself in five, ten and twenty years."

Twenty years? Noah couldn't even see clearly to tomorrow, let alone two decades from now. Charlotte and Cheyenne would be almost twenty-two years old. The same age their mother had been when he met her. He glanced over the seat at them. He'd run down any man who ever tried to get close to his daughters. *Whoa! When did that happen?* When did he go from the man who was dating girls to the man protecting his girls?

"I know that look." Fern clicked her tongue. "Gage had it when our kids were born. More so with Hannah. You're scared and you should be. You have a long and terrifying road ahead of you, Noah. But if you stick around long enough, you'll realize you're not in this alone. Believe it or not, we're here for you, too. I think you have a good heart and good intentions. They just might be a little misplaced at the moment."

Noah took comfort in her words. He'd never had a large family, but the brief time he had spent around Hannah's had taught him to respect and even envy her extended family support network to a certain degree. A few days ago, he had been certain taking his daughters home to Oregon was the right thing to do. Now he wasn't so sure he wanted to. Maybe they were better off in Ramblewood. But how could he leave them behind?

HANNAH AWOKE SHORTLY after midnight. Almost a week had passed since she brought the twins home. She'd insisted she didn't need her mom or Abby to stay over any longer and it was Hannah and the girls' first night alone. The conversation with Clay on the way back from the rodeo churned in her head. He'd been unsuccessful in his efforts to dig up any further information on Noah and had advised her to play as nicely as possible if she wanted to remain in the girls' lives. She'd had the same conversation with Avery, but she'd held out hope Clay would find something to use in their favor. In a way, she was relieved. She would hate for Charlotte and Cheyenne to grow up knowing they had a father unable to care for them because of some scandalous past. They deserved to have a relationship with him. It didn't make it any easier, though. The likelihood she'd retain full custody grew slimmer by the day. It wouldn't have been any different if Lauren were still alive and she'd found Noah.

She thought of a million chores she needed to do outside, but she didn't dare leave the children unattended. Not even with the high-tech baby-monitoring system Clay had installed when Lauren had moved in. She had never bothered to take the Wi-Fi cameras down from the girls' room, figuring they'd come home to visit.

Hannah shivered. The house still seemed cold without her best friend's laughter, even this early in the day. She dropped a paper filter into the coffeemaker followed by three scoops of ground beans. *Better make it four*, as Lauren would say when they were studying for finals. Hannah tried to swallow the sob that threatened to break free. She hadn't let herself truly grieve for fear she wouldn't be able to stop. Clearing her throat, she pressed the on button. "Keep it together, Hannah."

She marched into the living room, where she needed to start if she planned to pull off a successful Christmas. She reread the social worker's notes. *Repair floor.* The old peg and groove wooden floor was in dire need of refinishing, but Constance had only been concerned with three planks that had split and could catch tiny fingers. Clay had said he'd replace those today and the carpet company in town had a large beige remnant they would bind and have ready for pickup Monday afternoon. She'd considered wall-to-wall carpet in the room anyway, so covering the majority of the floor with an area rug until she decided if she wanted to refinish the floors had suited her fine. She'd asked the carpet guys to check for other remnants she could use in the dining room and upstairs hallways. She was open to any quick and cost-effective solutions. She'd spend her prize money before the end of the week if she weren't careful.

The owners of the rodeo school had been gracious enough to give her as much time off as she needed after they learned of Lauren's death. As much as she appreciated their support, it didn't pay the bills. She charged a monthly fee for the horses she boarded, but it wasn't enough. Competing in Vegas this year would have given her the money she needed, except leaving the girls for a week wouldn't help her custody case. Besides, she couldn't possibly desert them when they were still grieving for their mother.

The next item on Constance's list: *Radiator hazard.* The radiator had had a cover until Hannah broke it when she'd removed the covers to clean them. She'd been painting the living room anyway, and though she'd finished the walls weeks ago, she hadn't gotten around to replacing the damaged cover. Her dad said he'd take care of it. Painting the trim molding wasn't on Constance's list, but it was something she could do while the girls slept. Once the carpet was down tomorrow, she'd have another room completed and safe for the little tykes to play in so they wouldn't be confined to their bedroom and the sunroom The sunroom had been everyone's favorite spot in the house, since it overlooked the stables and corrals. It was also where Lauren had read to Charlotte and Cheyenne each evening and the place they seemed most at peace.

The long night faded into dawn as Hannah resealed

the paint can. It was almost seven. Time to wake the twins and get them dressed and fed before her family and friends arrived to help work on the house. She climbed the staircase to their bedroom and peeked in the partially open door. Cheyenne rubbed the sleep from her eyes while Charlotte stood in the crib, contemplating how to escape. She was more curious and exploratory than her sister. Always touching everything around her. Including Noah's face. She couldn't blame the kid. The thought had run through her mind on numerous occasions. Namely the night they met at Finnegan's Pub. Hannah had noticed Noah first and had been about to approach him when Lauren bumped into him at the bar. An actual bump, spilled drink and all. Within minutes, it was obvious her friend had fallen hard for the guy. The rest was history…or so they thought.

"What are you doing, little monkey?"

"Mommy!" Charlotte jumped up and down.

Hannah froze as déjà vu rocketed through her. Charlotte had that same reaction whenever Lauren had come home. Hannah knew Lauren wasn't behind her. She knew, but she looked anyway, wishing—praying—it had been a bad dream. The doorway was empty and Charlotte began to cry at the realization Mommy wasn't following her into the bedroom.

"It's okay, baby." She lifted Charlotte into her arms as Cheyenne silently stared up at them. Her sweet heart-shaped face watched, emotionless. She maintained eye contact while Hannah attempted to soothe her sister. Some response from her would have been better than none, but the child just watched and waited.

"Hannah?" Fern called from downstairs. "Honey, I'm here now. Do you need some help up there?"

Hannah knew her mother heard and saw everything from the baby monitor sitting at the bottom of the stairs. "I need more help than I realized, Mom," she admitted.

NOAH PARKED BEHIND Fern's SUV, hoping she'd already spoken to Hannah about him stopping by today. His ride back to Ramblewood with her yesterday had turned out better than he'd anticipated. He'd had the opportunity to spend time with Charlotte and Cheyenne and learn more about Hannah. "What are you doing here?" Hannah remained on the other side of the screen door, Cheyenne perched on her hip. In a matter of days, the girls' subtle differences had become more obvious to him. Charlotte seemed to always reach for him, whereas Cheyenne was much more uncertain if she wanted to be friends.

Well, that answered his question. "I take it your mom didn't mention I was coming over."

"Mom!" Hannah called over her shoulder. "Did you forget to tell me something?"

Fern pushed her way past her daughter and opened the screen door. "Hi, Noah. It's good to see you." She carried Charlotte in one arm while looping the other through his and leading him toward the kitchen. "Come on and have a cup of coffee and something to eat."

Hannah's cheeks puffed in annoyance. Noah shrugged, not quite knowing what to make of Fern's chipper demeanor. Charlotte stretched her tiny arm across Fern's chest and grabbed a firm hold of his shirt.

"Wait a minute." Hannah scooted past them and

blocked the kitchen doorway. "Will one of you start explaining what's going on here?"

Fern poked Hannah in the ribs, causing her to step aside, and then motioned for Noah to follow. "Stop being so melodramatic, Hannah." She pulled out a seat for him and plopped Charlotte in his lap. "Noah and I came to an understanding on the way home yesterday."

"We did?" Confused, Noah shook his head in an attempt to tell Hannah he had no idea what Fern meant. "We talked on the way back, but—"

"But nothing." Fern set a cup of coffee on the table along with cream and sugar. "I got to know more about Noah and I filled him in about you and our town…and Lauren."

"Mom, we're not a travel brochure." Hannah sat Cheyenne in the high chair and placed a colorful divided dish of fruit and what he assumed was some sort of cereal mixture on the tray. She strode into the mudroom off the kitchen and tugged on a pair of green knee-high rubber boots. "You two chat while I tend to the horses and the chickens." She smiled at Noah as he bounced Charlotte up and down on his knee. "I'd be careful if I were you. I just fed her and if you jostle her too much she'll—"

No sooner did she say it than Charlotte did it. Wonderful. At least it hit the floor and not his clothes.

"Welcome to fatherhood." Hannah laughed as her mother tossed him a roll of paper towels. "I'll be out back."

Fern lifted Charlotte out of his arms. "Hannah, aren't you going to help Noah?"

"No. A little barf is nothing when you're a parent. He's got this," she said. He detected a hint of a challenge behind her matter-of-fact tone. And that was fine—at least it was until the sour milk smell hit him. "Oh, then again, maybe he doesn't."

"I'm good." Noah stood. Queasy but good.

"You think that's bad, wait until you have to change a stinky diaper." Hannah laughed. "I'll have to record that for posterity."

"At least have some breakfast with us." Fern set Charlotte on a chair and began to clean her face. "Hannah's already painted the living room trim this morning. Such a busy thing. Around here, she does it all. I always had my Gage to help me when we had the sheep far—"

"Mom!" Hannah stared at her. "Stop forcing me down his throat."

Fern's sudden flirty attitude and singsong voice gave him the impression she was playing matchmaker. What was the old saying? If you can't beat them, join them. Somehow he didn't think Hannah subscribed to that same philosophy. At least not where he was concerned.

"Do you need any help?" Noah asked.

Both women turned to him. "I've got it, but thank you for asking," Fern replied. He meant Hannah, and judging by the look on her face, she knew it.

"I think we'll leave Egg Collecting 101 for another day." Hannah's genuine and throaty laugh came at his expense, but it was nice to hear. For someone who'd already worked on the house and wrangled two children and an overprotective mother today, she looked remarkably calm. He didn't know if he'd have the same reaction if this entire scenario had happened at his house. He couldn't even envision the girls there. He shook the thought from his head. It was because it was too soon. He hadn't adjusted to the situation yet. Of course they would fit in there. They had to.

By the time Hannah returned from her ranch chores, Noah had rehung two front shutters and was almost finished working on the second-floor banister with Clay. She squeezed past them on the stairs, leaving behind the scent of dirt and what he assumed was horse shit.

Clay caught him mid nose wrinkle and smiled. "Welcome to ranch life. Between mucking the stalls and the manure composting necessary for the organic farm, things tend to get a little ripe, if you know what I mean. You become immune to it after a while."

A door closed at the top of the steps, followed by the faint sound of running water. She reemerged less than fifteen minutes later, dressed, her damp hair in a loose braid, without a stitch of makeup. Not only was she the fastest woman in the bathroom, she was a knockout without any effort. *So this is what they mean by natural beauty.*

Clay cleared his throat as if reading Noah's thoughts. There was nothing like having an entire family and town around when you were trying to get to know someone…strictly for Charlotte and Cheyenne's sake, of course. He had no personal interest in Hannah whatsoever.

None.

He couldn't.

He did.

Hannah intrigued him. He had known Lauren's background, at least what he remembered of it after their encounter and from what Hannah had told him. Where Lauren had been more forward, Hannah was more reserved. She'd already told him she'd majored in agricultural science, but Fern had told him she had also minored in agricultural economics. Her mother had filled him in on all things Hannah yesterday, and he hadn't minded.

"How does she do it all?" Noah hadn't meant to ask the question aloud.

"My sister?" Clay gathered his tools and slapped him on the back. "My man, if you intend to raise twins, you better learn how to multitask real fast."

Noah sat on the bottom step. He could multitask. If he could hover over the tree line in a helicopter and maneuver logs dangling from a cable, he could handle twins. Couldn't he? He had years of training in the military and as a civilian. But Charlotte and Cheyenne didn't come with a manual and he didn't think the book he downloaded on his iPad last night would cover it.

Once again he found himself wondering if taking the girls home to Oregon was the best thing for them. "What am I doing?"

"I've been wondering the same thing." Hannah's voice startled him.

"Oh, hey. I was trying to figure out what to tackle next." Noah stood, inhaling her clean, fresh scent. *Much better.* "I'm surprised how many people are here."

"Lauren may not have been a Ramblewood native, but everyone loved her." Hannah motioned for him to follow her onto the front porch. She handed him a countersink and a hammer. "We need to make sure there are no raised nail heads out here." Hannah knelt beside him. "Lauren didn't have any family... none living anyway. She came home with me on weekends, holidays and during the summer. And when we rented our little apartment in town, she was involved in every community event...parades, festivals, you name it, Lauren was at the heart of it. Lauren *was* the heart of it. And everyone adores her girls. Everyone coming out here today isn't so much about helping me, it's about remembering Lauren and making sure Charlotte and Cheyenne have everything they need."

Noah easily envisioned his daughters growing up on the ranch. Not that he'd admit it to Hannah anytime soon. Maybe summers in Ramblewood wouldn't be such a bad thing.

Chapter Five

Monday morning, Hannah fought the urge to pace the lab's waiting room. Noah was a half hour late. Avery had insisted on an independent lab performing the paternity test for fear the hospital would notify social services, and the less Constance knew at this point, the better for Hannah. Avery would notify social services of Noah's paternal rights once they had a fully executed custody agreement in place. This way the courts would favor Hannah instead of relying on social services to determine temporary guardianship.

Technically Hannah could leave. The girls already had their mouths swabbed and Fern had taken them home. Avery had arranged for the lab to send the results to her office, so there was no reason for Hannah to stay—except for the inexplicable need to wait that gnawed at the pit of her stomach. She didn't know if it was out of fear or sympathy for Noah. It had to be fear, or maybe it was her own uneasiness.

The door swung wide and Noah ran into the clinic, out of breath. "I'm sorry I'm late." He patted his chest. "I got lost trying to find this place. The GPS in my rental is missing a few roads." He glanced around the room. "Where are the girls?"

"They already left with my mom. They got fidgety. What was I going to tell them if they started asking questions? There was no reason to keep them here."

The lines of concern on his face began to relax. "You're right. Can I at least see them later on?"

"I assumed you wanted to see them every day while you're here." Hannah didn't know how long he intended on staying in Ramblewood and hadn't asked for fear he'd try to take the girls with him. He had a job she figured he needed to get back to, as did she. In an attempt to reassure her that she'd have the girls for Christmas, Avery had explained that a custody agreement might take months to settle. Unfortunately, reassurance had become a foreign concept.

"Thank you." The receptionist slid the glass window open and handed him a form. He sat in the chair across from her, his pen tapping against the clipboard as he filled out the paperwork. "Why are you still here?"

Hannah twisted her thumb ring. "I don't know. I thought that maybe you needed a friend. I don't know who you've told about this or what kind of support system you have in place. And believe me, when you're a single parent, you need a support system. Lauren had a team of people rallying behind her. Since you don't know anyone else in town, I'm lending you a shoulder to lean on in case you need one."

He smiled nervously. "I'm assuming this won't take too long, and then we can be on our way."

Within minutes they called his name. William Knight.

No, it definitely didn't suit him. He looked more like a Noah. Strong and virile. Hannah watched the door close behind him. Okay, so the way his jeans hugged his backside as he crossed the room conjured up those images more than his name did.

More waiting. She'd never been a patient person. Like barrel racing, everything she did was at full speed. She had too much going on in her life to sit around. Her brother and some volunteers from Hanson's Hardware had been at the house when she'd left. The store had donated the supplies and they were prepping the old clapboards for a fresh coat of white. It hadn't been her first choice of color, but she'd worry about it years from now when it needed another paint job. She was overjoyed with any color offered. According to the social worker's report, the house needed to be free of peeling paint. Anything flaking off the walls presented a possible ingestion risk. If Hannah hadn't had so many people willing to help her, it would have been impossible to have her home ready for inspection at the end of the week.

Noah still hadn't mentioned his support system or his friends. She knew about his mother, but he hadn't talked about anyone else. It was inevitable Charlotte and Cheyenne would spend some time with him. She wanted—needed—to hear about the type of people who'd be in the girls' lives.

"That was painless." Noah interrupted her thoughts. "They said the results will take twenty-four to forty-eight hours."

And the waiting begins again.

Hannah thanked the receptionist and followed Noah to his car. "Do you mind if we stop at the dollar store on the way back? I want to pick up a few items so the girls can begin making Christmas ornaments and their gingerbread house." Hannah slid into the seat next to him. "Better yet, you can be in charge of the gingerbread."

"Me?" Confusion etched his features in an adorable way…much like Charlotte's. Another subtle reminder that the dynamics of their family unit were about to change. "How did I get roped into that one?"

She fastened her safety belt as he started the car. "Men build houses."

He draped an arm over her seat, checking the rear view. "Isn't that a little sexist?" His face was close to hers. Closer than it had been in the truck at the rodeo. The urge to kiss him reared its ugly head again. If she had turned away any faster, she'd have gotten whiplash.

"Yes, but in this case it works for me and it will be good practice for you." Hannah yanked her bag from the car floor, annoyed with the torrent of emotions running through her body. Was it lust? There was no place for any of that or anything else in their relationship except friendship. That was it. He was a new friend, if she could even call him that. "I just realized I don't have your phone number. Give it to me and I'll text you the link to the website Lauren got most of the children's projects and recipes from."

"They have a website for that?"

"I think they have a website for everything nowadays," she said. "Always check to make sure everything you give a child is nontoxic. Like you would never hand a kid any old marker and let them color with it. They have to use markers specifically formulated for children and preferably the kind that only write on special paper and not the walls and furniture, as Lauren and I found out the hard way."

"That had to have been fun."

Hannah laughed. "It wasn't when it happened. We walked into the living room and found Cheyenne covered head to toe in black marker, happily drawing on Charlotte. Our landlord was furious. We'd rented the place furnished and even though we'd painted over the walls with the help of five coats of primer, the marker refused to come out of the furniture. We never saw that security deposit again." She'd do anything to relive that day, despite the disaster. "I'm going to be honest with you." Hannah clasped her hands in her lap. "Your not knowing about kids frightens me. I'm not saying you can't learn. When the twins were born, my mom was right there beside Lauren 24/7 helping her and showing her what to do. How to diaper a baby. How to feed them. Plus, she went to prenatal and childcare classes. Lauren was super prepared and she still asked my mom for advice. You haven't had any of that and I'm not trying to belittle you, but what makes you think you can take the children home and know what to do?"

"I'll admit, the same thoughts have been running through my mind. I do have my mom, though, and I think she did a pretty good job with me, if I do say so myself." His grin was undeniably warm. "I also hope that you'll allow me to call you whenever I need to. And you can always visit."

She whirled to stare at him, fending off the quick anger that rose within her. "Thank you, but I don't want to be a visitor in their lives. I want to raise them, as Lauren intended." Her fingers dug into her hands as she resisted the urge to defend her place in the children's lives. Avery had warned her to keep her cool regardless of what he might say. She didn't think he meant to be a totally uncaring ass, and that wasn't the worst phrase that came to mind.

"I think we're getting ahead of ourselves. I haven't made any decisions yet, not that I even have a legal right to. Are you going to tell me where to go, or not?" He rested his forearms on the steering wheel and glanced at her sideways. "We've been blocking the exit for five minutes and now there's somebody behind us."

Good thing he clarified that last part, because she'd love nothing more than to tell him to go back to Oregon and stay there…alone.

She gave him directions and they rode the rest of the way in silence. When she went to step out of the car, he reached for her arm to stop her. "Tell me how you see this playing out."

Hannah sank into the seat. "Charlotte and Cheyenne have grown up with me and my family. We *are* their family. Legally and in every sense of the word." She shifted to face him. "If Lauren was still alive, she never would have let you take her kids away. I'm willing to give you what she would have given you—a couple weeks of vacation a year and vists whenever you want. But you'll be uprooting them if you force them to go to Oregon. You've acknowledged that Lauren's their mother, but you haven't granted me that same respect. Would you have taken the kids away from her?"

She was suddenly anxious to escape the confines of the car as a silence surrounded them. A cold knot formed in her stomach. She feared she'd said too much. She didn't want to anger or upset him, but she refused to allow him to ignore her role in their lives.

"I realize this situation is extremely unfair to you," Noah said. "I promise to take everything you're saying into consideration."

His unexpected response unsettled her. "I feel like I'm walking on eggshells around you. We can't get to know each other if we're constantly on edge. Avery already told me you won't get the girls before the holiday, so can we call a truce and give Charlotte and Cheyenne the Christmas they deserve?"

Noah's eyes shone with wetness as he nodded. "Yeah, I can do that. Go ahead on in. I need a minute."

His reaction surprised her. Hannah hadn't realized his attachment to the girls until now. She pinched the bridge of her nose. It had already happened. He'd fallen in love with them. She had no idea what made her reach for his hand and give it a squeeze. When he squeezed back, relief washed over her. They'd made some progress for the first time since he'd arrived. It was a start. The idea of spending Christmas with Noah both excited and frightened her. They were about to become a little family, giving Hannah the opportunity to show him the amount of love the girls had around them. Then maybe, just maybe, he'd give her the greatest gift of all—leaving Charlotte and Cheyenne with her.

NOAH'S PHONE HAD vibrated in his pocket repeatedly during their ride. He didn't want to be rude and answer it, especially since he suspected it was the attorney's office he'd contacted earlier. He retrieved the message and jotted down the information. He decided it was best to have this conversation when Hannah wasn't around. He didn't want to upset her further.

He felt like an ass. She had been right…again. He hated being wrong, especially when it came at his expense. She had assumed Lauren's role in the twins' lives. He didn't know if the law was in his favor, but he couldn't in good conscience hurt his daughters by separating them from Hannah. But that didn't mean he'd give up, either.

He opened the car door. Whatever the resolution was, he wouldn't find it today. He joined Hannah inside. She'd been in the store a few minutes and already held a basket filled to the brim.

"I'm ready to check out. You need anything?" she asked.

"That was fast."

"There are too many people waiting for me at the house. I can't waste time shopping. I needed to pick these up now so the girls could start working on their Christmas decorations." She held up her basket filled with colored paper, tape and stickers. "We enjoy making them together. I hope you'll join us."

Noah detected a twinge of apprehension in Hannah's jovial tone. Not that he blamed her. Christmas or not, she still thought of him as the enemy.

"I'll try my best. I haven't made decorations since

I was five or six years old." His mom was many wonderful things, but crafty was not one of them. "Now
that your parents' tree is all set, what about one for
the girls?"

"There is an organic Christmas tree farm not far
from the house and, depending on when we finish
today, I thought it would be nice to drive out there and
get one. I know the girls don't remember last year's tree.
And who knows if they'll remember this year's, but I
want them to have photos and videos to look at later. I
want them to know I—we—did our best to give them
an amazing Christmas under the circumstances."

Noah enveloped Hannah in a hug in the middle of
the store. And she hugged him back with her free arm.
Not only couldn't he lose his girls, he was beginning to
realize Charlotte and Cheyenne couldn't lose Hannah,
either. Somewhere his fight had changed from bringing
his daughters home to keeping a family together and
making sure he was a part of it.

BY THE TIME the sun began to set, Noah's body ached.
His heli-logging job required strict mental focus, not
physical strength. He hadn't been this sore since his
air force days. He could still run a six-minute mile and
maintained an active training schedule, of course. It
helped keep his mind sharp, but none of it involved
climbing up and down ladders, hefting shingles over
his shoulder or having two twenty-one-month-olds
bounce up and down on his chest as if he were a trampo-
line. He'd been away from home for a week and hadn't
worked out once.

When the dust settled, literally, he lent Hannah a hand damp mopping the floors and wiping down the walls. She was adamant about keeping the allergen levels to an absolute minimum while they made the repairs. The living room rug had been delivered and a plastic drop cloth hung in the doorway to keep further construction dust out. Now that the room was completed, he noticed how warmly Hannah had decorated it.

The light-coffee-colored walls contrasted with the white trim nicely. The room had a modern yet rustic feel. While she didn't have much furniture in here, the oversized and overstuffed couch and armchair invited you to sink into them. Instead of a coffee table, Hannah had laid out a washable play mat for the girls. The brick fireplace had a locking screen installed on the front of it to prevent little ones from climbing inside. Noah envisioned a tree in the corner and all three of them around it Christmas morning.

"It looks good, doesn't it?" Hannah came in, freshly showered. She flopped down on the couch. "We made more progress than I had expected today."

"You did a great job." Noah considered joining her but didn't think she'd take too kindly to him dirtying her couch. At least he'd had the good sense to kick off his boots. "I would have loved a room like this growing up. Honestly, I would have loved having this whole house and a big yard to run around in. I never knew my dad. He didn't want to know me or even pay child support. All my mom could afford was a tiny third-floor walk-up on the edge of town. It was neat and clean, but it only had one bedroom, which Mom selflessly gave to me while she slept on the couch. Not even a sofa bed. Just a couch. I look around this place and everything you've taken on, and it looks overwhelming to me, because as strong as my mom was and still is, I can't imagine her tackling this."

"Now I understand why you're so determined to claim your daughters. But you're not your father." She rose from the couch and crossed the room to him. "You're a better man than he is. Just keep in mind that even though I did the majority of this room on my own, I can't say that for the rest of the house. Sometimes being a parent means accepting help from others." She touched his arm lightly before moving the drop cloth doorway aside. "Are you hungry? I can reheat a casserole from the freezer."

"How about I clean up and take you and the twins out for dinner." Noah checked his watch. It was a little past six. "I think we deserve to relax, and then we can swing by that Christmas tree farm you mentioned."

"My mom fed the girls while we were working and I don't want to ask her to watch them again. She's been playing babysitter all day, every day for the past week." There was a trace of laughter in her voice. "Sometimes toting two kids to a restaurant is more trouble than staying home and cooking. Especially if you have to continually wrestle with them through dinner."

He stiffened. He ate out almost every night.

"Oh, looks like I hit a nerve." She raised her eyebrows in amusement.

"I know how to cook. I just don't. It seems pointless for one person when it's easier to grab a beer and a bite after work with my friends." His very single friends. "Guess I'll be breaking out the old pots and pans." Noah had to stop and think about when he had last boiled water. Between the microwave and pub, he didn't need to cook.

"How do you feel about lasagna? I think I have three of them. You're welcome to use the shower upstairs, unless you need to head to the hotel."

"I have a change of clothes in the car."

Noah slipped into his work boots and ducked outside. Fresh air filled his lungs. How did the atmosphere go from cozy to stifling in a matter of seconds? He removed his duffel bag from his truck. He'd traded in his rental car for a quad cab pickup earlier in the day so he could run any construction errand she might have. Besides, he'd felt a little emasculated having the only car—with the exception of Fern's crossover SUV—in a sea of trucks lined up across the front of Hannah's house. He drove a truck at home—he might as well drive one in Texas. His phone vibrated in his front pocket. He checked the caller ID—the attorney again.

"Hello?"

"May I please speak with William Knight?"

"Speaking. You can call me Noah. I go by my middle name."

"Noah it is. I'm Mark Fletcher. You left a message about retaining my services for a custody dispute."

"Hi. Mark, my boss, Frank Wallace, referred me to you." He lowered his voice and double-checked that Hannah hadn't come out on the porch before filling him in on the details.

"Has she retained an attorney?" Mark asked.

"Yes and I've met with her." A wave of apprehension surged through him. "She prefers to resolve this out of court. That is okay, right?"

"That would be the ideal scenario. Once we have the paternity test results, we'll have their birth certificates changed to reflect that you're their father, assuming your name isn't already on them."

"I don't see how that would be possible. She never knew my last name." He hadn't intended to make their night together sound cheap. He'd always preferred to remember it as a chance encounter, not a one-night stand.

"If you retain me, that's where we'll begin. I'll also need the name of her attorney," Mark continued. "Give me your email address. I'll send you over what I'll need and we can proceed from there."

"Sounds good." He hung up the phone feeling emotionally drained and somewhat deceitful. He didn't like going behind Hannah's back. He could head back inside and tell her about the phone call, or wait until they weren't about to eat dinner and buy a Christmas tree together. The latter option seemed smarter.

HANNAH HADN'T EXPECTED the organic Christmas tree farm to be so busy. They still had an hour before they closed. She'd debated between getting a live tree and an artificial one, but she couldn't fathom Christmas without the scent of a tree permeating the air.

Hannah lifted Charlotte out of the car seat and into the stroller despite her protests. Both girls had been fidgety and they hadn't even made it past the parking lot. It had been unseasonably warm today and Hannah had probably overdressed them. She fastened Cheyenne into her side of the stroller. The little girl's aloofness continued to concern her. Cheyenne had begun communicating less with everyone, including Charlotte. With the exception of jumping on Noah for all of maybe a minute earlier, she hadn't played very much, either.

If she didn't show some emotion by next week, Hannah would consult their pediatrician. She'd read that children their age grieved in their own way. Where Charlotte had become clingy, Cheyenne had withdrawn into a protective shell. Her mother had noticed it, too.

"Are the two of you hot?" She bent over the stroller and unzipped both of their sweatshirts. "There, that should help."

Charlotte grabbed hold of Noah's jeans. "Oh, hey there, sweetheart." Noah crouched down in front of them. He lifted both of their hands to his lips and gave them a kiss. Charlotte giggled and squealed. Cheyenne watched without a sound.

The girls needed an established routine again. With the exception of breakfast and bedtime, they bounced back and forth between her house and her parents'. Hannah also couldn't help but wonder if Noah's inclusion in their lives had happened too fast. They were used to him being around the majority of the day and she wondered how they would react when he left to go back to Oregon. They probably already wondered who he was.

"I think I know the answer, but I'll ask anyway." Noah stood. "Why an organic tree?"

"It all goes back to my allergies. Between the fungicides, herbicides and insecticides they spray the trees with, my throat would actually begin to close. That's when my dad started cutting down a tree from our own property. Every spring he plants a new one to replenish what he took. I feel it's important to keep those toxins away from the girls, especially when you never know what they'll put in their mouth next."

"You've definitely given me something to think about. I'm sorry you went through all that as a child." His voice was soothing. "Your parents must have been terrified of losing you."

"How about we choose a precut tree and head home." It wasn't really a question. The evening had begun to feel too family-like, and while spending time with Noah like this was deliciously cozy, it did a number on her nerves. Especially after their borderline romantic dinner. Well, as romantic as frozen lasagna could be.

The twins had watched *Yo Gabba Gabba!* on TV while she and Noah had a conversation that didn't revolve around the girls. She'd enjoyed listening to his air force stories, envisioning him in his first lieutenant uniform. He'd told her more about his job and what it was like spending his days above the rest of the world in a helicopter. His taste for country music had surprised her. She'd pegged him for more of a hard rock type. He'd even been interested when she showed him her organic farm business plan. And when he admitted that he wanted to try his luck gathering eggs tomorrow morning, she almost fell off her chair. The more he had opened up to her tonight, the more drawn to him she became. But falling for the father of her best friend's children wasn't right.

"I don't know." Noah looked around. "I kind of wanted to cut down a tree for you and the girls the way your dad did."

No, no, no. Don't say something romantic!

"I didn't grow up with that experience," Noah continued. "We had a fake tree and store-bought decorations."

That's better. "Then let's find ourselves a tree." Hannah pushed the stroller past him until his hand covered hers, strong and firm. She took a calming deep breath and inhaled his fresh, crisp scent. Almost citrusy, but not quite. Whatever it was, it was raw and intoxicating. *So much for calming.* Why hadn't she detected it in the truck? Because his chest hadn't been pressed against the back of her shoulder.

"Allow me." His lips were so close, her hair moved as he spoke.

She gripped the stroller tighter, for fear if she let go she'd melt into a puddle on the ground. *This can't be happening.* The more they had talked over dinner, the more she saw Noah the person and not just a potential threat. Being around him heightened her senses and left her feeling protected at the same time. She didn't need to feel like this. She could take care of herself. She could take care of the girls herself, the same way Lauren had. But now she could picture him there beside her as she did. In her home, in their lives.

Hannah released the stroller and grabbed the bow

saw from him, letting him take the lead. She followed, noticing once again the way his jeans fit his backside perfectly. She groaned.

"Did you say something?" Noah glanced over his shoulder.

"No." She ran ahead of them and pointed to a tree. "What do you think of this one?"

"I think it looks good. What about you, girls? Do you like it?" Charlotte was too busy attempting to unfasten her seat belt while Cheyenne watched. Noah's brows rose. "Tough crowd." He bent down behind the stroller. "Is there a way to secure this thing?"

"The brake is right here." Hannah slipped between him and the stroller and pressed the pedal down with her foot.

Noah looked up at her from the ground and smiled warmly. "Thank you."

Please don't smile. "Here." She thrust the saw handle at him, knocking him off balance as he attempted to grab it before it tumbled to the ground. She reached out to stop him from falling and landed on top of him. His arms encircled her, one hand resting on her bare skin at the small of her back. The comfort of his embrace drew her close. A little too close.

Hannah's heartbeat sped up in time with his. His eyes dropped to her mouth as he moved even closer. If ever she wanted a man to kiss her, it was now.

And then she heard it. The distinctive click of the stroller's seat belt.

She pushed herself off Noah and scrambled on her knees to the front of the stroller before Charlotte's feet hit the ground. "Oh, no, you don't." She swept the toddler up in her arms and rocked her, staring at Noah. "Whatever just almost happened can never happen."

Chapter Six

They rode to the ranch in silence. Partly because the girls had fallen asleep, partly because if they spoke, they'd have to acknowledge the kiss that almost happened. Noah smiled. He hadn't realized how badly he wanted to kiss her until she pulled away from him. He knew what he would be dreaming about tonight.

He parked the truck near the front porch and hopped out. "Why don't we trade vehicles for the night?" Noah said. "That way we don't have to switch the car seats again."

She lifted Charlotte into her arms. The child stirred, then drifted back off. "You don't like my truck much, do you?"

"It's not that. I love old trucks." The '72 Dodge had long since forgotten what color it was and could stand a tune-up, but it seemed roadworthy.

"It's bought and paid for. Despite a few unexpected backfires here and there, it runs pretty good. It's not great at trailering horses, but I can borrow my dad's or Clay's trucks when I compete. It's perfect for farming."

Therein lay the problem. It was for farm use, not

toting around two toddlers. Maybe that was why he hadn't seen Hannah take the girls out in it since that day in the cemetery.

He carried Cheyenne into the house and followed Hannah and Charlotte upstairs to the bedroom. He'd peeked in the room earlier after he'd showered but hadn't had a chance to look around. Painted the same yellow as the sunroom, it was cute without being too girlie. The color reminded him of a baby duckling. Two white cribs stood in the far corner. On the opposite wall, a white dresser was lined with framed photographs of Lauren. Hannah lifted Cheyenne out of his arms and settled both girls in a single crib and joined him.

"She was beautiful, wasn't she?" Hannah asked.

Noah nodded. The woman in the photos was a distant memory compared to the past week with Hannah.

"This—" Hannah waved her hands from him to the cribs "—should have been you and Lauren putting the twins to bed."

A heaviness settled in his chest. "Is that how you picture it? Lauren and I together, living happily ever after? Because I don't and I don't believe she did, either. If she had held out hope, her will would have mentioned me and her wishes if I happened to come into the children's lives one day. You said it yourself. She left because she was embarrassed. Sleeping with a stranger wasn't her style. I was a mistake with very real consequences. I'm glad she tried to find me, and one day she may very well have succeeded. But it wouldn't have had a fairy-tale ending, Hannah."

"Why don't you ever ask me about her?"

"Because I don't want to play the what-if game. I do that enough when it comes to the girls, I don't want to do it with Lauren, too." His voice broke. "I have to keep reminding myself not to live in the past. I can't regain the twenty-one months I've lost. Besides, you have filled me in on quite a few things about Lauren. I'd rather learn more about her through her daughters."

"Do you think you would've dated her if she'd given you her phone number that night?" A look of sorrow crossed Hannah's features.

"I don't know. Maybe." Noah carefully chose his words. "I don't care much for long-distance relationships. I'm also not big on one-night stands. Granted, the night began with a few too many drinks, but I would've liked to have seen where it went." Noah shifted from one foot to the other, realizing he'd forgotten to take off his boots when he entered the house. "I thought we had a strong connection when we met." He hesitated, measuring her reaction. "But it wasn't strong enough for her to trust me with her phone number. She didn't feel the same way."

Noah crossed the room to the girls' crib. They were so small and fragile. He'd do anything in the world to protect them. Hannah had been wrong the other day when she said he wasn't a father yet. He was...100 percent.

"I don't know what's happening between you and me, but whatever it is, it's completely different from my brief time with Lauren. I enjoy getting to know you, even though we don't always agree," he whispered. He walked out of the room and waited for her to join him in the hallway.

She turned on the baby monitor and closed the door before angrily shooing him down the stairs. He waited for her in the foyer. "Why are you upset with me? I'm trying to be honest about my feelings for you."

"You're not allowed to feel anything about me or for me." She attempted to walk past him, but he reached for her waist and tugged her to him.

"Why not?" He smoothed her hair back from her face, grazing her soft skin with the back of his hand.

"Because Lauren was my best friend." Grief and longing reflected in her eyes. "She was my sister at heart and I could never betray her that way."

"If there was something special between me and Lauren, it ended that morning." Noah felt her body stiffen against his. "We spent eight hours at the most together and we spent the majority of that in bed." Hannah twisted out of his arms before he could stop her. "I don't mean to sound crude or callous, and I certainly don't want to disparage Lauren in any way. I've asked myself repeatedly—as I'm sure she did—how much of that connection was sexual." Noah hated admitting any of this to Hannah. "Come on, you know what I mean. Lust and love can be hard to separate or distinguish when you first meet someone."

"No, I don't know. I've never been in love." Hannah's cheeks stained a dark red. "I was always too busy with the rodeo and school. I never found the one I wanted to commit my life to. I don't believe in falling in love with multiple people. When the right man comes along, I'll know."

Noah sat on the bottom step. "I'm not going to pretend I don't feel something between you and me. Maybe it does have something to do with our situation. I'd like to explore it, though. And I respect that my being the father of Lauren's children affects your feelings toward me. Those eight hours I spent with her changed all of our lives. There's no time limit on grief. You may never look at me the way I look at you, and that's fine. It won't change the way I feel about Charlotte and Cheyenne. Just know I'm here for all of you."

Hannah leaned against the doorway of the dining room, arms folded, averting her eyes.

"I'll go get the tree." As Noah stepped outside, he fully expected her to lock him out, but she left the door open.

He pulled his flannel shirt tightly across his T-shirted chest. A crisp breeze had replaced the heavier warm air. He strode over to the truck bed and removed the Christmas tree. The organic tree farm's operation had surprised him. They'd had a mechanical tree shaker to ensure all the critters were out and a net baler to wrap the tree for transport. He wouldn't mind owning that business if it ever became available. Especially now that he was learning the importance of a chemical-free environment for his daughters and Hannah. It was still logging, in a roundabout way.

What was he thinking? He had no intention of moving to Texas. None. Right? It would be different if they had heli-loggers in the heart of Hill Country. He'd be a fool to give up his salary for any reason.

His hesitation scared him. He'd known Hannah and the girls for six days and he was already wrestling with emotions he hadn't experienced before. This wasn't a good sign. Or was it a great sign? He was in constant tumult in their presence, especially Hannah's. He was in Ramblewood to establish paternity and…and what? The plan kept changing and he desperately needed to settle on one before he lost the best thing that ever happened to him.

HANNAH WATCHED NOAH from the entryway. Reeling with confusion, she didn't want to face him, yet she was unable to walk away. She had no business feeling anything for the man, but tonight had been one continuous battle with herself. She had a glimpse of what a future with Noah and the children would be like— together as a happy, idyllic family. He felt it, too. But was it really hers to have?

Everything Noah had told her about him and Lauren replayed in her mind. Lauren *had* been the one to walk away. How much of a connection could there have been when she'd made a point of disappearing? Lauren had regretted her decision only after she found out she was pregnant.

"Where would you like it?"

"Huh?" Her breathing halted as her pulse quickened.

Noah stood in the open doorway, kicking off his work boots while holding the Christmas tree in one hand and the stand in the other. "I gave it another fresh cut. Where do you want me to set it up?"

"Uh…um…" Hannah's brain short-circuited. "The corner of the living room, to the left of the fireplace so you can see it from outside."

Noah's gaze searched hers. "Are you okay?"

"Of course." Hannah hurried past him and pulled the plastic drop cloth aside so he could get through the archway. She ran to the corner, her arms wide. "Here would be perfect."

Noah stared at her. Her body tingled under his scrutiny. "Sweetheart." He half laughed. "If you want me to put the tree there, you're going to have to move out of the way."

Hannah slinked away from the window. What the heck was wrong with her? Noah wasn't the first man she'd wanted to kiss, although none of them had been rugged, ex-military helicopter pilots who'd helped create two of the most beautiful angels on earth.

Rather than risk embarrassing herself, Hannah escaped into the kitchen. She filled a watering can, composed her thoughts and returned, maintaining a safe distance from Noah.

"You beat me to it." Noah reached for the steel can. "I wondered where you ran off to."

She hadn't run off. Okay, she had. "I wanted to stay one step ahead of you." That was the truth. "I think we should call it a day. It's late, the kids are in bed and I need to get up early. Here are the keys to my truck. I'll take you up on your offer. I'm not planning on going anywhere tomorrow, though."

"Mine are by the stairs." Noah filled the stand and took the keys. "What time do we collect eggs?"

She laughed. "You were serious?"

"Why not?" He handed her back the can. "I'm open to new experiences."

Hannah narrowed her eyes. "You are, huh?" She could teach him a thing or two. "Be here at five. You can stay here with the kids while I tend to the horses, then once they're up and fed—which you can do—I'll put you to work in the henhouse."

"*Work* in the henhouse." His left brow rose the same way Cheyenne's did when she was leery about something.

"You'll see." A renewed confidence swept over her. She was an expert when it came to her ranch. And she may be in the midst of an emotional upheaval, but she was confident in her ability to turn the plans for her land into a reality. Even if it took every ounce of strength she had, she'd ensure Charlotte and Cheyenne were there beside her. If Noah wanted to be part of their lives, he'd have to figure out how to do it in Ramblewood. It was time for her to regain control.

NOAH KNOCKED ON Hannah's front door at five minutes to five.

She opened the door barefoot, dressed in faded denim overalls, a long-sleeve gray T-shirt, and her hair up in a messy bun. Country casual shouldn't look so sexy this early in the morning. "I wasn't sure you'd show up. Come on in."

"Here are your keys. Your truck wasn't half bad. Well, once I realized I wasn't being shot at."

Hannah laughed. "Old Blue can scare a calf out of a cow from ten miles away when she gets temperamental. She runs a little rough in the morning."

Ah...so that's the color of the truck. "That's one way of putting it." He slipped off his boots and carried them to the back of the house, leaving them in the mudroom off the kitchen. "Is the porch getting painted today?" he asked as she handed him a cup of coffee.

Hannah nodded. "The painters are using a sprayer, so it won't take long, but we won't be able to walk on it for a few days. I hope it's dry in time for Friday's inspection." *We?* Noah wondered if she included him in her *we*. A piece of toast popped up in the toaster and she grabbed it, pointing to the loaf of bread on the counter. "Help yourself to whatever you want. People are still dropping off food." She bit off a piece, dry. "The kids are asleep and the baby monitor is on the table. Take it with you wherever you go. I'll probably be finished by the time they wake up." Hannah scrutinized him. "You're not a diaper man, are you?" She laughed. "We're not quite ready for potty training. Lauren had start—" She waved her toast. "Nope, I am not going to make myself cry. Holler out the back door if they wake up and I'll walk you through the process. I'll be in the stables mucking stalls. Then we'll—you'll—tackle the eggs." She tugged on a pair of boots over her bare feet and bounded down the back steps.

Picking up the baby monitor, he ran his fingers across the screen, resisting every impulse to go upstairs and hold his daughters. They needed their sleep. He clipped the monitor to his belt and watched Hannah through the back door.

She began opening the outer stall doors, allowing fresh air to enter the stables before disappearing inside. Every so often, he'd see her reappear in one of the stalls. Somewhere in the distance, he heard the sound of a small engine start. A large puff of smoke appeared as Hannah drove a battered red tractor pulling a wooden trailer filled with hay bales. She stopped in front of a large metal rack in the middle of one of the pastures, cut the engine and climbed onto the wagon.

After cutting open the bales, she filled the rack with hay using a large pitchfork.

"Oh," Noah said. "They're horse feeders."

She repeated the process in two more pastures before returning to the stables. Within minutes, she led two horses down a dirt path and into a pasture behind the barrel racing practice area. After she'd turned out the rest of them, she pulled a pair of gloves from her pocket, grabbed the wheelbarrow next to the stables and disappeared.

Noah walked back into the kitchen, feeling guilty for not helping her. Being idle was not his strong suit. His stomach growled. He glanced around the kitchen. The room was an organized chaos of food. When he spotted the half-eaten cherry pie in the fridge, he knew what he was having for breakfast.

After washing his empty plate, he tiptoed upstairs and peeked in at the girls. Seeing them on a three-inch black-and-white screen just didn't cut it. Cheyenne was sound asleep on her back and Charlotte was curled up beside her. He'd have to remember to ask Hannah later why the girls slept together when they had two cribs.

The marvels of creation fascinated him. It didn't matter how many times he saw the twins, he still couldn't believe they were real. Maybe the paternity test results would help solidify that feeling.

He resisted the urge to look in Hannah's room before making his way downstairs. He wanted to learn more about her, but he wanted to discover who she was organically. Noah laughed to himself. One week around Hannah and he was talking about organics.

He hadn't meant to find the social worker's report, but it was hard to miss nailed to the pantry door. Hannah and Clay had filled him in on what they needed to complete. A few days ago, it had sounded like an insurmountable list, but with the exception of the porch, she was finished.

The dining room had become a construction material catchall. He could work on straightening it up. He wanted to go outside and explore the ranch but couldn't leave the twins. An hour later, he felt slightly more useful. A truck rumbled out front. The painters had arrived to spray the porch. He plodded through the house to let Hannah know. He hadn't expected to find her pushing a wheelbarrow full of manure to a large fenced area he figured was a compost heap.

"She maneuvers that thing like a boss," Noah said to himself. She impressed him more every day.

Hannah took a five-minute break, spoke to the painters and then went back to work. Noah wanted to get out there and help, not be stuck inside waiting to hear a cry on the monitor. He had a strong suspicion that had been Hannah's point. Back in Oregon, he came and went as he pleased and Hannah knew it. She'd shown him the meaning of *tied down* in a matter of hours. The concept would take some getting used to.

Hannah finished her chores and showered before the girls awoke. Diaper duty officially became his least favorite part of parenthood. He'd diapered the right end. That had to count for something.

"How do you plan to do all of this on your own?" Noah asked, more out of fear he wouldn't be able to do it on *his* own.

"I told you. I have help. A lot of it. You know that old saying that it takes a village to raise a child? It's true, especially when there are twins. I don't know how Lauren did it alone in Boston. Her new job had on-site day care. She could pop in and see them throughout the day and that made a world of difference. That's why she accepted the position. What would you do with them in Oregon? Get up in the morning, drop them off at day care for eight to ten hours and then pick them up at night when they're too tired to have anything to do with you? Why do you want some stranger raising your kids when my family and I are here?"

He didn't have a response. In a perfect world, he wouldn't hire a stranger. He would hire…Hannah? He wondered if she'd be open to the idea of coming with them to Oregon as the girls' nanny. Of course, she'd be more than hired help. While the idea had its appeal, he didn't think Hannah would go for it. If she would at least give Aurora a chance, she might want to move there. She could do everything she was doing in Texas, only there. It would be a big change, but it wasn't impossible. Then they could parent the kids together.

After a breakfast of flying fruit and played-in cereal, he didn't know who needed a change of clothes more. How he'd ended up wearing the twins' food was beyond him, but he was exhausted by nine in the morning.

"Ready for the chickens?" An amused expression crossed her face. "We're already behind schedule."

"We are?" Noah thought they'd done pretty well. She was challenging him and he relished every minute of it…sans diapers. Her mood had noticeably lifted since yesterday evening and he was enjoying her lighter side. "Lead me to them."

"Grab the stroller and meet me outside." Hannah had the kids up, ready and outside before he'd managed to get the stroller open. "Come on, big guy. I have faith in you," she mocked from the back steps.

"This isn't fair." Noah found the release and the stroller sprung into shape, almost taking out his manhood in the process. "You had directions the first time you did this."

Once the kids were fastened in the stroller, they walked to the henhouse. "They're loud."

"Cackling means they're laying eggs. I check them twice a day." She parked the stroller outside the whitewashed structure. "I have roll-out nest boxes, so all you need to do is lift this lid and collect them."

There were probably thirty brown and white eggs sitting atop a green artificial grass-like material. "What's the difference between the two?"

"Nothing. The color of a chicken's ears determines what color eggs they lay."

"Chickens have ears?"

Hannah stared at him incredulously. "Of course they have ears." Hannah opened the outer pen gate, picked up a chicken and held it up to him. "Look right here."

"I'll be damned. I never knew chickens had ears."

Hannah swatted him. "No swearing around the kids."

"What did I say?"

"*D-a-m-n-e-d.* We don't use that language when little ones are present."

"I'm sorry." He'd never considered the word a swearword before. "What's my punishment?"

"You're going to clean the henhouse." Her smile lit her face brighter than the midmorning sun.

"I'm what?"

"Hannah rested her hand on his back and gave him a gentle push. "Go inside and shoo out the hens. Don't be afraid of them." She handed him a pair of gloves. "Shovel all the soiled bedding into a wheelbarrow. There's a large scraper hanging on the back of the henhouse door. Scrape down the floor to make sure it's chicken-poop free. Dust all the corners and nooks with the broom to make sure there aren't any spiders or snakes lurking around."

"Snakes?" Noah hadn't signed on for snakes.

"They love to dine on eggs." Hannah patted his arm. "You'll be okay. The broom will protect you," she teased. "If you see a snake, call me and I'll take care of it. Keep your hands out of any dark recesses and you'll be fine. After you're finished with that, I'll show you how to put down fresh straw, and then you'll clean and disinfect the food and water dishes with the poultry-safe disinfectant hanging on the door next to the scraper. We'll feed them, and then chicken duty will be over for the morning. I'm going to take the girls to see the horses and will check on you in a little bit."

"You do this every day?"

"I like to clean out the coop once a week. It's been almost two with everything going on."

When he offered to collect the eggs, he hadn't expected to be roped into cleaning up after the hens. He carefully opened the door and looked in. He couldn't remember ever being around chickens. It wasn't as if he lived in the city, but you didn't usually stumble across a chicken in a helicopter. A bird jumped at him from the corner flapping its wings. He screamed and closed the door.

"That's quite a girlie scream you have going on," Hannah called from the path between the corrals. "They're more afraid of you than you are of them."

"You want to bet?" he mumbled. After a few false starts, Noah managed to clean the henhouse and ruin his boots at the same time. By the end of the morning, he wanted to join Charlotte and Cheyenne when they went down for a nap.

Hannah told him more about her plans for the farm while they ate lunch. Her cell phone rang and Hannah answered. "It's Avery," she whispered to him. "The paternity test results are in." She listened while nodding.

"His attorney?" Astonishment lit her face. "I hadn't realized he had one. I assumed he would, but no, he hadn't mentioned it."

"About that." He'd planned to tell Hannah that morning but hadn't had the opportunity. He'd transferred the retainer fee through his mobile banking app last night and had expected it to take a day or two before the funds were processed and Mark contacted Avery. "I was going to tell you."

Still on the phone, Hannah strode to the pantry and tore the social worker's list off the wall. "It will be finished today, with the exception of cleanup." She paced the room. "Okay, we'll see you later. Thank you." She hung up and pocketed her phone. "We have to meet Avery at her office at five o'clock."

"If she has the results now, why can't she read them to us over the phone?"

"They're sealed and she won't open them until we're there and she has your attorney on the phone at the same time."

"She can't do this sooner?" He'd no doubt the twins were his, but he wanted to see it in black and white.

"She has other clients. Five o'clock is the soonest." Her right hand tapped wildly against her thigh. "What happens now?"

Noah understood her apprehension. "We take it one step at a time. I wanted you to hear about my attorney from me, not Avery. There wasn't a good time this morning."

"When did you hire him?" She shot him a penetrating look.

"Last night."

A soft gasp escaped her. "Wow! I feel like a fool. Here I thought we were getting closer. At least that's what you led me to believe. The joke's on me."

Noah swung her into the circle of his arms, refusing to allow her to think he'd played her. He lifted her chin so she'd look at him. "We are getting closer." His lips brushed hers. It was a simple, sweet kiss until she entwined her fingers in his hair, pulling him closer with her free hand, and kissed him the way a man dreamed of being kissed.

"Noah." Her voice was barely a whisper against his mouth.

His lips softly found hers, easing them apart with his tongue. Slow and easy, he drew her to him. She stood on her toes and wound her arms around his neck. He'd dated his fair share of women, but none had curled his toes and made his blood boil at the same time. And damned if he didn't want more of it.

His hands found her bottom and lifted her onto the edge of the counter. He broke their kiss and gazed at her. Her lips were swollen from the assault, her eyes hungry. "Tell me to stop and I will."

"The children are upstairs." Breathless, she tilted her head back and looked toward the ceiling.

"They're upstairs sleeping. The workers are finished painting the porch and it's just you and me." Her rapid pulse was visible on the side of her neck. His hands traveled up her thighs, pausing on her waist. His thumbs gently grazed the tender bit of flesh beneath the hem of her shirt. He was thankful she'd shed her loose overalls for something more formfitting after her shower.

"Wait." She pushed lightly against his chest. "How do I know you're not just attracted to me because you feel it will help you with the girls?"

Noah eased her down from the counter. "I would never use you that way." He pulled out a chair for her at the table and sat across from her. "I could ask the same question. I know you're grieving and I probably shouldn't have kissed you, but I'm finding it more and more impossible to deny what's developing between us. And please don't ask me what I would do if Charlotte and Cheyenne weren't part of the equation, because they are. I choose to live in the present and look toward the future. I'd like to see where it leads with you."

"I need more time. We're about to hear proof you're the girls' father. And you're right. I need to be certain what I feel for you is really about you and not because I'm terrified of losing them."

It pained Noah knowing she lived in constant fear of what he might do. And he kicked himself for not being more sympathetic to her needs sooner. "I want you to be a part of their lives."

Hannah covered her face. "Wait until after we meet with Avery to tell me that."

"Okay." Noah stood. He could give her time and space to process the torrent of emotions she was experiencing. "I can wait."

Chapter Seven

Why did I kiss him?

Hannah parked alongside Noah's truck in front of the attorney's office. She wrapped her arms tightly around her midriff. The kiss had set off spirals of euphoria throughout her body, awakening parts she hadn't known existed. The tension between them had shattered. And then as soon as the kiss had ended, it reappeared with a vengeance. She chose not to ride with him to Avery's office to give herself time to think. Abby had offered to watch the twins, giving Hannah time to absorb the information she was about to receive.

She willed herself out of her truck, flattening her palm against Noah's hood before going inside. Ice-cold. He'd been there for a while. Foreboding gripped her heart. The paternity test had only been a formality. Without the results, Noah was powerless. In a few minutes, he'd have the ammunition necessary to change Charlotte and Cheyenne's lives forever. At least the girls would gain a living parent out of the deal.

Noah rose as she entered. She sat next to him, wishing the chairs weren't so close she could smell his shampoo.

She refused to make eye contact, but even in her peripheral vision, he managed to look good.

Avery dialed Mark Fletcher's office. After a round of introductions, she tore open the envelope from the lab. Noah took Hannah's hand in his. Her instincts told her to pull away while fear screamed at her to hang on. Their fingers entwined as Avery read the results aloud.

"William Noah Knight, you are Charlotte and Cheyenne's biological father." Avery handed him the report and shook his hand—the one not holding Hannah's. "Congratulations, you're officially a father."

Well, that was anticlimactic. Hannah's stomach clenched tight as her mind attempted to register the significance of the results. "Congratulations." Hannah forced herself to stand. She held out her hand, but he hugged her instead.

"Congratulations, Noah." Mark's voice boomed from the speakerphone. "I'll begin working on having your name added to the birth certificates. I'll call you tomorrow to discuss the matter further. Avery, thank you for your time this evening. Hannah, take care."

Discuss the matter. Take care. In other words…kiss off, Hannah.

"Noah, would you mind giving me a minute with my client?" Avery asked.

Elation slid from Noah's face. "I don't want this to turn into a war." He took Hannah's face in his hands. "I want to raise my babies, with you."

"How is that possible?" She gripped his wrists. "We live in separate worlds, two thousand miles away from one another. Our lives don't intersect. I'll compete once a year in Oregon and you'll conduct a seminar or two in Texas, but that's it. There's nothing more."

"There has to be." His brows drew together.

"Hannah?" Avery's voice was thick with concern.

Hannah edged to the door. "Avery, I'll call you tomorrow. Noah, please give me space tonight. Tomorrow we will tell the girls, together."

She waited until she was out of their view before she ran. She couldn't get down the law office stairs fast enough. Christmas lights shone bright from lampposts and storefronts, bathing the street in red and green.

Christmas was less than a month away. She should be spending her time planning the best Christmas possible. This year Charlotte and Cheyenne were old enough to appreciate the day. This year they would understand who Santa and Rudolph were. This year they would miss their mom. And this year might be the last Christmas Hannah would spend with them. Her throat ached as she fought the sob that threatened to break free.

Any control she thought she had earlier had vanished. She had a legal document connecting her to the children. Noah had blood. She feared the courts would give him the advantage. She had two choices—convince him to stay in Ramblewood or scare him away from fulltime parenthood. In order for either of those to happen, he needed to spend more time with her and the twins. Could she ask him to move in with them temporarily?

That came with one major downside. He was now well aware of his effect on her. She'd strengthened her guard since their kitchen incident and she'd like to think she was fully immunized against his charms. As long as he kept his hands—*and mouth*—to himself, she'd swallow her pride for the children's sake. The arrangement would also give her a chance to observe his daily interactions with the children. She couldn't imagine him saying no. Until the girls were legally taken from her, she had time.

Hannah climbed into her truck and relaxed against the seat. If he moved in, she might be able to keep her promise of raising the girls after all.

NOAH HATED THE WAY things had ended with Hannah yesterday. He'd picked up the phone to call her numerous times but hadn't dialed. She'd asked for space and he would give it to her. Besides, he had his hands full trying to figure out how to tell Charlotte and Cheyenne he was their father. He'd rehearsed it in the mirror a hundred times since midnight. He wasn't sure how much they understood. He didn't want them to see him as a replacement for their mother. No one could take Lauren's place. Hannah came close, but she'd never consider herself a replacement.

He checked his watch. It was almost seven o'clock. He'd been up since three debating what time he should head to her house. He'd spoken with his boss last night and filled him in on the latest details. While Frank was sympathetic to the situation, he also had a business to run. Helicopter-logging pilots were extremely specialized. Not many people could do what he did. They had hoped to bring in a temp from British Columbia, but that had fallen through. Noah had to fly home tonight.

Noah grabbed his jacket and headed to the ranch. Fern greeted him from the screen door.

"Stop right there," she said before he reached the bottom step. "The paint is still tacky. You have to use the back door."

Whew! For a second there, he thought Hannah's mother was banning him from the house. She had the mudroom door open before he turned the corner. He spotted Hannah in the stable entrance, a shovel in her hand. He waved, receiving only a nod in response.

A loud cackling rose from the henhouse.

"Has she collected the eggs this morning?" Noah asked Fern.

The woman shook her head. "Not yet."

"I'll be in shortly." Noah took a basket from the pile next to the coop, flipped open the lid of the nest boxes and collected the eggs. Twenty-seven. He figured it was the least he could do to help. He'd felt like an ass last night when he realized he hadn't contributed a single cent to raising his children. He knew the attorneys would start hashing out a child support amount, but he felt Hannah—no, Charlotte and Cheyenne— deserved a lump sum now. He had no idea how to attach a dollar value to twenty-one months, but he owed them something.

When he finished with the eggs, he laid out fresh water and food for the chickens. It was one less chore for Hannah. He cleaned up and joined Fern in the kitchen, who somehow had managed to feed the girls without their flinging food everywhere.

"We're all getting a late start around here today."

Fern set a heaping plate of bacon and scrambled eggs on the table. "Help yourself."

Noah had been so nervous earlier he'd forgotten to eat. He fixed himself a plate and sat across from the twins in their high chairs. This morning he could unequivocally say they were his daughters.

He made them.

He thought he understood what that meant before. He'd known from the moment he saw them that they were his. But the gut feeling hadn't compared to the unequivocal DNA proof they were his. Any sliver of doubt lurking in the background had vanished. He officially understood a parent's love for their children. No other feeling compared. When he looked at them, his heart felt full. Truly full. That had been a foreign concept until today.

Before his smile gave him away, Noah popped a forkful of eggs into his mouth. "Oh, my. Fern...these are the best eggs I have ever had." He closed his eyes and savored their creaminess. He never knew scrambled eggs could be this exquisite. They were light and fluffy and—

"You all right there?" Hannah stood in the doorway of the kitchen. "Do we need to give you some privacy?"

Noah's eyes flew open. "I was just telling your mom how amazing the eggs are."

"That's because you've always eaten store-bought, overprocessed food. This is what organic farm fresh food tastes like." Hannah washed her hands in the sink, grabbed a plate and joined them. "With the exception of the past week and a half, we eat very cleanly around here. Lauren was a big believer in clean living, too."

"I can see why. I've traveled around the world and I have never experienced farm fresh anything before. I can understand why you love this ranch. I don't know much about organic farming, but this is amazing. I'll miss eating with you like this."

"Why does that sound like you're leaving?" Hannah rested her fork on the plate's edge. "Mom, could you take the girls to the sunroom, please?"

"As long as you two promise to behave." Fern lifted Cheyenne out of her high chair. Noah rose to help her, but she brushed him off. "I've been juggling these two since the day they were born. You go on ahead with your chat."

Noah sat down and scooted his chair closer to Hannah. "I am leaving, temporarily." He kept his voice low. "I need to fly home today."

"I hope you don't think you're taking the girls with you." Her lips thinned.

"Of course not." Noah leaned back and rubbed his temples. "I wish you'd give me more credit. Legally I can't take them anywhere. I'm needed at work. Hopefully it will only be for a few days. It might be longer. I'd rather stay here and work this out, but I can't. I have two new tiny humans to support and I can't afford to lose my job."

"Fine." Hannah cleared the plates from the table without taking a bite from hers. "Since you're leaving, you can't tell them you're their father today."

"Why not?" Noah shot up from his chair, almost

knocking it over. "I have waited a week at your request. I refuse to wait another day."

"Why do you want to confuse them?" she demanded. "They had a mom and she's gone. Now here's Dad, but he's leaving in a few hours. You just said you don't know when you're coming back. Tell them when you know you'll be around for a while. They've lost too much already."

He scrubbed his hands over his face. She had a point. Telling the twins he was their father was more for his benefit than it was theirs. If they were older, he might argue his point further. "Fine, I'll wait. I've waited this long. Will you let me spend what little time I have today with them?"

"Of course."

"Please don't hold the paternity results against me. Nothing has changed. We both knew what the results would be."

"That's not true. There was still doubt, however slight. Everything is changing. Again." Hannah ran her hands up and down her thighs. "I have a proposition for you. Since it will take some time to resolve the custody issue, how would you like to stay here whenever you're in town? I could use the extra hand with the girls, my mom could use the break, we could get to know each other, and Charlotte and Cheyenne could get to know you."

"You want me to stay here with you?" Living with Hannah and his daughters sounded too good to be true.

"This arrangement has nothing to do with you and me. It's strictly about our relationship with the girls. You can have Lauren's old room. It's still fully furnished. But touching, kissing…any of that is off-limits. Think you might be interested?"

Noah didn't need to think. It was the perfect solution. "You have yourself a roommate."

LATER THAT DAY, Hannah hung up the phone. Noah had called after he arrived home in Oregon. They hadn't had a lengthy conversation, but she'd detected sadness in his voice. What would happen once the girls knew he was their father? Their relationship with him would grow, but they'd be more upset every time he left. They'd been heartbroken when Lauren had gone to Boston for a few days to interview at the pharmaceutical company. Cheyenne had refused to eat and Charlotte had developed a new habit of throwing everything within her reach.

Hannah had allowed the girls to sleep in this morning. For the first time in over a week, their lives weren't revolving around the construction crews' schedule. The girls had needed the extra rest. Cheyenne had even become more sociable with Noah today. It would be interesting to see her reaction tomorrow when he wasn't around.

Thanks to her brother's help with the ranch that afternoon, she found time for a long soak in the tub. Afterward, she collapsed on the living room couch. It had been quiet when Lauren moved to Boston, but Hannah had had projects to keep her constantly busy. Now the house was silent. Too silent.

Hannah didn't want to hear the word *project* for a long while. *Burnt out* was a phrase she'd just become acquainted with. She flipped through the television channels. Nothing piqued her interest. Her eyes were too heavy for reading, but she wasn't tired enough to fall asleep. One thought repeatedly churned in her head. Noah was two thousand miles away.

"I think I miss him."

She felt guilty for it, too. She'd spent a week with Noah. Some days they were together from sunup to sundown. Lauren hadn't even spent a whole day with him. That was reality. The logical side of her brain told her it was okay to want more of a relationship…to be more than just roommates. She'd had a taste of the passion they shared, and if he hadn't stopped, she wouldn't have, either. She remembered his hands on her body. He made her feel alive, and after losing Lauren, feeling alive and living meant more than it ever had. *Everyone says life is short, but unless you've lost someone too soon, you have no idea.* She hadn't understood until now.

Hannah picked up her phone and redialed her last incoming call.

"This is unexpected." His voice exuded warmth, cocooning her in a blanket of instant comfort. It had been only a couple of hours since they'd spoken, but it felt more like days. "Is everything okay?"

I'm lonely and I miss you. "Everything's fine." Hannah allowed herself the goofy grin plastered across her face, since no one else could see it. "I had an idea, though."

"Should I be worried?"

She detected a hint of mischief in his question. "I

hope not." She giggled...actually giggled. She wasn't a giggle girl. "Do you have video chat on your phone?"

Noah's deep sensuous laugh traveled through the airwaves and straight to her core. "What do you have in mind?"

"Get your mind out of the gutter." Hannah cautioned herself not to buy into the inflections in his voice, or the way they reverberated in her ear as if he were standing beside her. *Damn!* "I thought maybe you could video chat Charlotte and Cheyenne tomorrow when you got off work."

"That's a great idea."

Hannah didn't need to see his face to know he was smiling. "Wonderful! I think it will help them accept you in their lives if they can see you every day."

"Do you want to try it now?"

Yes! "Sure, but the girls are already asleep."

"I know they are. You told me when I called you earlier. I want to see you."

Hannah ran a hand over her hair. She wasn't exactly glammed up, but the man had already seen her at her worst. So why was she so nervous? It was a conversation, nothing more. Despite her weak attempt at logic, her hand trembled as she activated the phone's camera.

"There's your beautiful face. Not that I could ever forget what you look like."

Noah's chiseled features filled the small screen. His blue eyes were darker, more mysterious than they'd been in the warm Texas sun.

"I look like a million other girls out there." Hannah

was acutely aware he was studying her as closely as she studied him. "Don't blow smoke."

"I'm not." His expression stilled. "If I say any more, you'll argue with me and I think we've done enough of that."

"I think so, too." Okay, video chatting with Noah was kind of awkward. She'd done it a million times with her friends and family, but tonight she wasn't sure if she should sit or stand or what to do with her other hand. Staring at his face the entire time made her body uncomfortably warm. He had a great face—an amazingly kissable face. She groaned. *This isn't working.*

"What's wrong?" Concern etched his features.

"Truth?" She might as well put it out there.

"That would be nice." There was that irresistibly devastating smile again.

"I—" Hannah cleared her throat. "I'm trying to figure out how to do this—whatever this is—with you. I'd like to explore it further."

"Ah, our kitchen tryst." His eyes widened at the memory.

"Hardly a tryst, Noah. It was a kiss. A damn good one." She felt the heat rush to her cheeks. Hopefully the room was dark enough to hide the embarrassing assault. "That is, if you're still interested?"

"Sweetheart, I'm very interested." Noah's eyes smoldered with intensity as he stared at her through the screen. "I don't know what the future holds or how all of this will work out, but I don't think either of us will regret trying."

"Noah." A passionate shiver of desire surged through

her. She wanted to feel his arms around her, his mouth against hers. She wanted the one man she shouldn't. The only man who'd made her body tremble in anticipation of their next meeting.

"We'll figure this out, Hannah." His voice, thick and steady, tempted her to explore the possibility of a future together.

"I hope so." Hannah feared she'd say more than she should if they didn't end the conversation. "I've kept you on here long enough. And I'm getting tired. I wish I could sleep in like the girls."

"You deserve to have someone take care of you," he said with gentle emphasis.

"I don't need anyone to take care of me, Noah."

"I'm not saying need, I'm saying deserve. There's a difference. Maybe when I'm there, you'll let me do that for you."

She wished she could alter time. Since the night of Lauren's accident, she wanted to turn it back. Now she foolishly dreamed of wasting it, so it would fly by. She reminded herself to enjoy the moment. The kids were asleep upstairs and Noah was in front of her, even if only on a screen. For a brief moment, they were together. And that meant the world to Hannah.

NOAH WANDERED AROUND his house after he hung up with Hannah. He used to love the modern structure. He'd spent years designing it, carefully planning the cement floors and counters in every room. The built-in furniture and overall utilitarian vibe starkly contrasted the glass exterior walls overlooking the Willamette River.

The property was private and secluded. And it was lonely and cold.

He'd almost kicked off his shoes when he arrived home from the airport. It seemed the most natural thing to do in Hannah's house. The wood floors and carpet were warm and inviting. He had no desire to walk barefoot on his cement floors. He'd been home for almost two hours and he felt chilly and damp. The house had plenty of heat. It just didn't have any heart. Hannah's had been all heart even when it had been a construction nightmare.

He looked around his living room. He couldn't picture the twins playing on the floor. The hard floor. Even if he had an area rug, it would still be hard and cold. And heaven forbid one of the girls fell on this floor or whacked her head. It pained him to admit it, but his house was not child friendly. A social worker would never find anything structurally wrong with it, but he couldn't picture them feeling overly positive about it, either. The property itself was another story. He didn't even have a yard for the girls to play in. He had trees, and a steep drop-off down to the river.

Noah sat on a stainless-steel stool at the kitchen counter. Nothing felt comfortable anymore. Before he left for Texas, he'd loved everything about his house. He'd loved coming home to it. It had been his sanctuary. Now his furniture seemed foreign. The paternity lab had exuded more warmth than this place.

He'd begun with a very singular plan. Bring his girls home. Between Hannah and the legal system, his plan had detoured through an organic horse-filled ranch and a henhouse. So he'd considered another plan, one where he attempted to convince Hannah to move to Aurora. His sardonic laugh echoed off the walls. She'd hate the house. *I hate the house.* He hated it because his daughters would never belong in it. They would never forgive him for taking them away from their comfortable surroundings.

The thought of a place in the suburbs made his skin crawl. A few weeks ago, he'd probably have said the same thing about living on a ranch. But what if he could find a ranch where Hannah could have her horses and her farm? How could she say no?

Noah grabbed a notepad from the drawer. He had to speak with his attorney and find a real-estate agent. He jotted down everything he needed to do before he could bring his daughters home. His list seemed more daunting than Hannah's had been. Her house had been a lot of work, but at least she could rest easy and enjoy having the children live with her for the foreseeable future. There had been an effortlessness around Hannah and his daughters despite the superficial frustrations. Changing his entire lifestyle to accommodate them almost seemed unfeasible. He wanted to go home but wasn't quite sure where that was anymore.

NOAH WOKE GRUMPY the following morning. When he was in Ramblewood, he looked forward to getting up and seeing the girls. This was nuts. He loved his job. Hovering a twelve-ton helicopter the size of a bus just above the treetops was exhilarating and challenging. He had to plan out every movement, especially when his loads outweighed the helicopter itself. But as thrilling as it was, it didn't compare to being a father to two twenty-one-month-old toddlers.

Noah climbed behind the wheel of his red Dodge Ram. He didn't have the heart to tell Hannah he had a much newer version of her truck. He grabbed a doughnut and coffee in town, already missing Fern's scrambled eggs and bacon. He even missed flying fruit and cereal.

"Hey, man, it's good to have you back." Frank slapped him on the shoulder. "When are you going to bring the little ones home?"

"It might be a long while. I need to talk to you about my schedule. I have to be able to spend time with my kids, especially at Christmas."

An hour later, Noah and Frank had hashed out a tentative three-and-a-half-day workweek schedule. Noah had off Thursday afternoons through Sunday. It looked great on paper until he factored in the five-and-a-half-hour flight plus the travel times to and from the airports. Never mind that the weather in the Pacific Northwest had the potential to decimate the plan with one storm. Flying one of the largest heli-logging aircrafts narrowed the pilot field down even further. He was only in his Chinook making lifts and drops for an hour and a half a day. The rest of his time he spent flying smaller helicopters to run errands and transport ground workers in and out of the woods. It was easy finding someone to fly those, but his copilot was still in training and didn't have enough hours to operate the Chinook just yet, which put an enormous strain on his boss. Noah felt good climbing into the cockpit. He soared over the tree line until he spotted his ground crew. He checked his long line and lowered the hook. Once they hooked him into the choker they'd wrapped around the tree, he waited for the crew to clear the log and then was up on his way to the drop zone less than thirty seconds later. He flew over the zone, and with a click of his thumb, the hook opened and released the log. Within minutes of picking up the first load, he was back for another. This was his element. Up in the sky he was in total control. His job may be one of the most dangerous in the world, but it didn't compare to the danger his heart was in when it came to Hannah and his daughters.

IF HANNAH EVER thought she had been nervous before, she'd been seriously mistaken. She'd been awake since two in the morning, checking and rechecking the house to ensure it was ready for Constance's inspection today. She hadn't given a specific time, but Hannah prayed it was soon. Between the copious amounts of caffeine she had consumed and the twins' dislike for the outfits she'd chosen, her nerves were just about shot.

Her family had arrived before sunrise, providing both moral support and a united front. She still hadn't decided if having her family there was a blessing or a curse. She feared Constance wouldn't think she could do it on her own if she had to have a team of people rallying behind her. Those thoughts were short-lived, dying as soon as Constance drove up. Hannah was thankful she had her family there. She'd never needed them more.

After a two-hour inspection, Constance joined Hannah, the twins and her family on the front porch. "Miss Tanner, I'm almost speechless," the social worker began. "You completed everything on my list and then some. You have an extraordinary support system in place here and I couldn't be happier to see that. Congratulations on a job well-done."

Hannah had managed to keep it together until Constance left. She thanked her family and then excused herself to the stables. She saddled Restless, mounted and rode. The back of her property faced state land, giving her the freedom to travel the numerous trails carved out by other riders through the years.

She didn't want anyone to see her cry. Passing inspection had been bittersweet. All it did was guarantee she would have Charlotte and Cheyenne until Noah decided to take them away. She wanted to put all her trust in him and believe he wanted them to be together. She wasn't accustomed to being at anyone's mercy, and while he may argue that fact, she had no other way to explain how she felt.

Hannah's phone rang in her pocket. She reined Restless to a stop and looked at the screen.

Noah.

"Hello," she answered.

"Hey, sweetness." His voice instantly made her belly somersault. "I wanted to see how you were holding up."

"Great, actually." Hannah should have called him as soon as the inspection was over. They were his daughters and he deserved to know the status of their living arrangements. "Constance left a little while ago. Everything passed."

"I knew it would." Noah's voice remained even. "Now you can relax."

Hannah's sudden burst of laughter caused Restless's ears to prick and his body to shift suddenly. "Easy, boy." She patted the side of his neck. "You're okay."

"I hope you're with a horse or a very young boy."

"Jealous?" Hannah sucked in her bottom lip, awaiting his response.

"A little. And curious, now that you ask. Should I be worried?"

"Should I?" Hannah's breath stilled.

"Have faith we'll figure this out. Together. I want what's best for my girls and that seems to be you. We'll talk more tonight, okay? I need to get back to work."

"Be careful up there." She pocketed her phone and steered Restless back the way they'd come. "Everything's going to be okay." She nudged the horse into a trot, finally allowing herself the freedom to celebrate today's accomplishment. For the first time since Lauren's death, she had hope.

By MIDAFTERNOON, NOAH called it. The winds had picked up and conditions had become too treacherous to fly. They'd have to try again tomorrow. After retrieving the last of his crew from the forest floor, he headed home for the night, forgoing their usual pub routine. A freezing rain had begun to fall. As he reached for the four-wheel-drive control switch, the back tires lost traction on the frozen highway. He spun the wheel in the opposite direction of the skid to regain control. He swore under his breath as he merged into a makeshift lane behind a line of cars and attempted to steady his erratic pulse. Ice began accumulating on the windshield faster than the wipers could sweep it away. The front defroster offered little help in keeping the windows clear. He was seven miles away from home. Seven miles away from a video chat with Charlotte, Cheyenne and Hannah. He couldn't afford an accident…not now that he had family to look after.

The SUV in front of him fishtailed wildly. He tapped the brakes and felt a hard thud from behind, causing the rear of his truck to kick out, sending him sideways down the highway. His breath caught as he fought to maintain control. Headlights fast approached the passenger side. Noah spun the wheel again. For a moment, he felt weightless, as if he were flying one of his helicopters, then the truck came to a sudden stop on the shoulder. For a brief second, he questioned if he'd survived. He looked behind him to see that multiple vehicles had collided and he'd somehow escaped unscathed.

Hannah had feared his daughters would lose another parent because of his job. Instead, he'd almost lost his life the same way Lauren had. An icy chill passed through him and he wondered if she'd been his guardian angel keeping him safe for the family waiting for him in Texas.

Chapter Eight

Whoever said absence makes the heart grow fonder needed to be slapped. It had been over a week since she'd last seen Noah in person. They video chatted every night, sometimes during the day, depending on their schedules, and Noah had even begun reading the girls their bedtime stories. The situation wasn't perfect, but it worked.

She checked herself in the mirror one last time. Okay, for the twentieth time. It was late Friday evening and Noah said he'd arrive before midnight. He was supposed to arrive yesterday, but a storm in Oregon had shut down the airport for twelve hours. She'd checked his flight—twice. It had landed almost two hours ago. She'd expected him to call once he picked up his rental car, but he hadn't. She'd received a one-line text message instead saying he was on the way.

Hannah checked on the girls before heading downstairs. They still slept in the same crib. She tried separating them every night, and after a few hours of temper tantrums, she gave up. She didn't see the harm in them sleeping together, but they needed more room. They'd be twenty-two months old in a few days and Hannah felt it was time to transition them into bigger beds. Charlotte had already managed to climb out of the crib twice. Hannah had installed a baby gate at the top of the stairs when she first purchased the house. Even though the social worker said it had passed inspection, Hannah had gone ahead and replaced it with a much higher one the other day. She feared if the twins made it past the gate across the bedroom door, they'd scale the other and tumble down the stairs. Trying to keep up with their inquisitive minds kept Hannah awake most nights.

Headlights bounced off the far wall of the room. She looked out the window and saw a pickup truck pulling down the drive toward the house. *Noah.* She closed the door and quickly tiptoed downstairs, not wanting to wake the girls. They'd grown more accustomed to Noah every day through their video chats and had begun anticipating his next call. She ran out on the porch to greet him, barefoot in the chilly night air. He'd parked at the bottom of the stairs. "Hi."

"Hi, yourself. I'm sorry I didn't call. My battery was about to die and all I packed was my wall charger." The outdoor sconces on both sides of the door bathed him in a radiant golden light. Noah slung his black duffel bag over his shoulder, exposing the fitted navy blue T-shirt beneath his vintage bomber jacket. His chest muscles flexed as he climbed the stairs. Thank God it wasn't daytime, because if he'd been wearing aviators she'd be a puddle on the floor. The man was rugged to the core. A small cell phone screen did not do him justice. She wanted to pull a Charlotte and run her palms over his stubble, luxuriating in the feel of it against her bare hands. "Hannah? I asked you how you are."

"What?" She snapped to attention. "I'm good."

"You sure?" He searched her face. "You looked like you were someplace else there for a minute."

I was. She hadn't meant to ogle him…well, at least she hadn't meant to get caught doing it. "Sorry, the girls' room is right above the porch and I was thinking about not waking them."

"Oh, good point." The corners of his mouth lifted invitingly. "In that case, we should go inside." He looked down the length of the porch. "I love the scarecrow Mr. and Mrs. Claus. Did you make the Christmas sweaters?"

"That was all Abby. She loves to knit." Hannah and the twins had more sweaters than they could possibly wear during their short Texas winters. "Be careful. If you sit still long enough, you might end up with a Christmas sweater of your own."

"Thanks for the warning." His eyes dropped to her feet and he smiled. "Believe it or not, I've missed your toes."

"Excuse me?" Hannah started to laugh at the unexpected comment.

"My house isn't exactly a barefoot kind of place. I got used to kicking off my boots with you. Wow, that sounded corny." For the first time since they'd met, his cheeks darkened and Hannah found the vulnerability endearing. "Love the horse-head wreath on the door."

"Thank you." The pine creation with its red ribbon halter and miniature pinecone decorations had delighted the girls when her sister-in-law brought it over the other day. "Abby again. She's the crafting queen."

"Are you going to invite me in?"

"Of course!" she said louder than she'd anticipated. "Come in."

Hannah wished she'd thought to turn on the foyer light before heading outside. The faint glow from the living room lamps provided a whisper of illumination, leaving her to stand in the shadows with Noah mere inches from her grasp.

"I didn't just miss your toes. I missed all of you." His voice, intoxicating and deep, sent a shiver of desire down her spine. Before she had a chance to respond, his mouth sought hers as his arms wrapped firmly around her waist, pressing the length of his body against hers. The caress of his lips left her breathless. And then he released her—much too soon, for she'd barely been sated.

Hannah blindly reached for the newel post to steady herself. "Wow." The faintness of her voice mirrored the weakness in her limbs. Clearly, he didn't need to wear sunglasses to melt her resolve. "Where in heaven's name did that come from?"

After their relationship conversation the day Noah had left, neither of them had mentioned it again. They hadn't had a chance between legal updates and constant toddler activity.

"Did I offend you?" He laughed quietly.

"No." Hannah hurried into the living room. It was safer…brighter. She would see him coming this time— if he attempted to kiss her again. The thought alone warmed her insides. "The topic of us hasn't come up in a while, so I wasn't sure if you still felt the same way."

Noah shrugged off his jacket in the foyer and draped it over the banister. Holding her gaze, he knocked off his boots and swiftly crossed the room to stand in front of her. "Tell me you don't want to see where this goes and I'll never press the issue again. I promise I won't hold it against you or cut you out of the children's lives."

Hannah bristled at the last part. "As if you could." She stepped away from him.

A cloud of sadness settled upon his features. "I had hoped you'd realize by now that I would never hurt you that way. I've apparently failed to convey the message, and for that, I apologize. But I will not apologize for wanting you." He slid his hands into the pockets of his jeans almost shyly, as if he'd exposed more of himself than he'd intended.

Hannah wanted him to wrap her in the safety of his arms; she wanted to open her heart to him completely. There was too much at risk and she had to take their relationship slowly. The twins' future depended on her and she couldn't let her desire for Noah overshadow that responsibility.

He exhaled, opening his mouth as if to say something, then closing it. He glanced at the Christmas tree in the corner of the room and smiled. "The tree looks good."

"The girls make a few ornaments every night. By Christmas Eve it will be full."

Noah lifted the baby monitor from the end table and ran his fingers across the screen. "They're so precious.

I can't believe I'm in the same house with them again. I was beginning to wonder if I'd been dreaming."

"You can go up and see them if you'd like." Even if they woke, Hannah was confident he'd be able to soothe them back to sleep. "They missed your chat tonight. They didn't ask, but Cheyenne took the phone a few times. I think her little internal clock sensed it was past when you usually call."

"You sure it's okay?" he asked, halfway to the staircase.

"Of course." She settled onto the couch, tucking her legs beneath her. "Just be forewarned, there's a new gate at the top of the stairs requiring two hands and brute strength to open."

"You're not coming?"

"No, this is your moment with your daughters." As he ascended the stairs, she closed her eyes, enjoying the warmth of the house. She heard him fumble with the gate, followed by a low thud. She figured he'd chosen to go over it instead of through it. The floorboards creaked overhead. She smiled and nestled down into the overstuffed pillows, comforted by the sound of his soft whispers to the children as they slept. Noah was home.

"Good morning, beautiful."

Noah sat on the edge of the couch and gently shook Hannah awake. She stretched languidly, arched her back, then bolted upright and looked around the room. He winked at Charlotte and Cheyenne, who waddled over and climbed up beside her.

"What time is it?" She gave both of them a hug and

a quick kiss on the top of their heads while trying to see out the window. "It can't be morning already. I have so much to do." She attempted to scoot out from under them. Her legs wobbled as she stood.

"Relax." He reached up and placed his hands on her hips to steady her. "The coffee is already made—although you really need one of those single-cup brewers. I had forgotten how to make coffee the old-fashioned way," he teased. "The girls have been fed and dressed, in case you haven't noticed. And I collected the eggs. I would've cleaned out the henhouse, but I didn't want to leave the girls in the stroller for that long."

Hannah's adorable wide-eyed expression made him want to kiss her. If the girls hadn't been in the room, he might have.

"For the record, I can't afford those individual coffee cup things, plus they're bad for the environment. I can't believe you did all of that for me." She looked down at the girls. "Where did those clothes come from? I've never seen them before."

"I bought them." Noah stood Cheyenne on his lap and tugged on the bottom of her bright green shirt with a large reindeer head on the front. "I couldn't resist the candy cane striped pants."

"Leggings," she corrected. "And they're adorable. How did you know what size to buy?"

"Between my mom and the store clerk, we had it covered." The outfit was how he broke the news about the girls to his mom. He'd asked her to go shopping with him to pick up a gift for a friend. It hadn't been his brightest idea. He'd forgotten to consider her reaction, which was a mix of elation and a safe sex speech. "I took so many photos of the girls when I was here, and they were able to guess their size."

He'd already sent his mother a photo of them in their new clothes. She would have preferred to see them in person and had even hinted about joining him, but he didn't want to spring his mom on Hannah just yet.

"You bought them socks, too?" Hannah smiled down at the little green toes. "I'm impressed. What did you make them for breakfast?"

"There was a bowl of cut-up fruit in the fridge, and I mixed them up that cereal I watched you make the day I helped feed them. That was the right thing to give them, wasn't it?"

Hannah look shocked. "Absolutely. I hadn't realized you were taking notes."

"You shouldn't have to do it all, Hannah." He respected her strength and determination. A lesser woman would have faltered under the pressure.

"You give me too much credit. My mom helps out quite a bit."

"I wondered if she would stop over this morning." Despite their disastrous start on Thanksgiving, Noah enjoyed spending time with Fern.

"I told her not to bother, since I knew you would be here. I still don't know what time it is."

"Almost nine. What do you have planned for today?"

"I need to feed and turn out the horses and then muck their stalls. I'm usually done with that by now." Hannah bounced her foot anxiously. "I promised the girls we'd take them to the Winter Festival and then to see Santa. I figured while we were in town I would stop in at the furniture store and look into some children's beds. They've outgrown those cribs, especially since they insist on sleeping together."

"I hope you'll allow me to pay for the beds."

Hannah opened her mouth to protest, then quickly closed it. "Thank you. That would be wonderful."

"I owe these two a good deal of child support. I know the attorneys will figure it out, but until then please allow me to pay for whatever they need. Whatever you need, too."

"I can take care of myself, but I won't turn down help for them. I'm not that proud."

"Then tell me what I can do to help you today." He followed Hannah into the kitchen.

"Just watch the girls." She scanned the room. "I can't believe you even did the dishes. I'll finish up as fast as I can so we can get there before the Christmas parade."

A little after noon, Noah drove his newfound family into town. A few weeks ago, he was a happily single man with no responsibilities outside of work. Today he had a family. All he needed was a dog and cat to complete the picture.

The streets of Ramblewood were brimming over with Christmas. Hand-painted window displays enticed shoppers to step inside while flags adorned with holly and candy canes swung in the gentle breeze outside their doors. Banners were strung across the street, wishing everyone a Merry Christmas and reminding visitors to attend the Mistletoe Rodeo.

"Are you competing in that rodeo?" Noah asked.

"Yes. All the proceeds go to the Ramblewood Food Bank, so the competitors don't win any prize money. Instead, local businesses donate prizes. Most of my students will be there. For some, this is their first competition. They'll have a chance to win saddles and horse tack. The rough stock competitors—the ones riding the bulls and the bucking broncs—are competing for everything from boots to a horse trailer this year. This is the second year they've held the event. I'm super excited to see my students out there. I was glad to get back to work last week and see them all."

"Where are the girls when you teach?" Noah winced. He hadn't meant his question to sound so accusatory. "Let me rephrase that."

"It's okay." Hannah smiled up at him and he wished she'd slip her arm through his as they walked down the street. "I understand your concern and you have every right to ask. This time of year I only have one class in the afternoon, after my students get out of school. My mom comes over and watches the girls. I'm not gone long."

"Based on what I've read about your career, you're one of the top barrel racers in the country. Weren't you supposed to go to Las Vegas for some competition this week? What happened with that?"

"The National Finals Rodeo. And yes, I was supposed to be there. Barrel racers compete the entire year in order to qualify. That prize money at the end of the year makes it all worthwhile." Her smile slid from her face. "But life happens and it wasn't the best time for me to leave the girls with my parents. They would've happily watched them, but I didn't feel comfortable with it. You have to make sacrifices when you have kids."

Noah hadn't realized how much Hannah had given up for the children. And she didn't complain. She cared for them as if they were her own. It touched him that somebody could love a child that wasn't theirs. He was probably more jaded than most, considering he grew up without a father.

They decided to eat lunch at the Dog House, where servers with puppy ears and tails served them Christmas hot dogs decorated red and green with ketchup and relish.

"I wish you could have been here for the tree lighting ceremony last night." Hannah cut up the girls' food. "These two had a blast. We sang Christmas carols and had hot chocolate with marshmallows. And the grade school—" her face brightened "—they put on an amazing show with more singing and dancing. I can't wait to see the twins up there in a few years."

"It's sounds wonderful. I'm sorry I missed it." Noah chose to ignore her comment about the girls staying in Ramblewood. Of course, she would still feel that way. She hadn't been to Aurora yet and they hadn't settled custody. The girls had been assigned a guardian ad litem, but they were a long way from a resolution. Besides, once he found a ranch for Hannah in Oregon, she'd realize how dedicated he was to making their co-parenting relationship work. Of course, he wanted more, but he'd settle for that to begin with. He still didn't know how to broach the subject of the ranch to her. Once she saw where he lived, met his mom and friends, and saw how much he loved his job, how good he was at it, she would understand why he couldn't move to Texas. "Hey, you two." Noah turned his attention to the girls. "Have you written your letters to Santa yet?"

"Not yet." Hannah wrinkled her nose. "I still don't think they understand who Santa is. I hope once they see him today they'll be more excited about writing him a letter. There are a few Christmas specials on tonight we can watch. They saw *Frosty the Snowman* the other night and they cried when he melted, which made me cry. Then again, I still cry when the spider dies in *Charlotte's Web*."

"You?" Noah wiped the ketchup from Cheyenne's face. "The same woman who armed me with a broom and told me to take out the spiders in the henhouse?"

"Those spiders aren't cute. Charlotte is."

"Speaking of Charlotte." He ruffled the girl's hair. "Do their names have any particular significance? How did she choose them?"

"Lauren didn't even know the answer to that question." Hannah turned away from him and stared out the window. "I went with her to her first ultrasound." Her voice softened at the recollection. "That was the day she found out she was having twins." She inhaled sharply and swiveled back to him. "On the way back to our apartment, she began talking to her stomach and called the girls Charlotte and Cheyenne. She never had any other names for them. She didn't even know if they were boys or girls or one of each. She just knew that they were a Charlotte and a Cheyenne. Cheyenne can go either way and if both of them turned out to be boys, she would have named the other Charlie."

"I like the name Charlie. Does anyone ever call Charlotte that?"

"Not yet." Hannah shook her head. "We talked about nicknames and figured the kids would decide what they liked once they were in school, much the same way you did with your name."

It surprised him whenever he heard that Lauren's thoughts were similar to his own. He had barely known her, and here he had two beautiful girls with the woman. They probably would have coparented together very successfully.

"I know I'm probably asking this question too soon, but did Lauren dream of their pursuing a certain profession, like a doctor or a lawyer? My mom always figured I'd be a pilot because I was fascinated with planes, even when I was younger than the girls."

"Not really. She used to say that whatever Cheyenne grew up to be, she hoped she made a lot of money because she'd probably have to repeatedly bail Charlotte out of jail."

"I can definitely see that." Noah laughed. "They have two very distinct personalities."

"That they do." Hannah rose from the table and gathered their food wrappers. "We need to get going. People are already beginning to line up on the sidewalk."

Noah enjoyed pushing the twins' stroller down Main Street with Hannah by his side. If he had known having a family would feel this good, he might have done it sooner. But then it wouldn't have been this family.

Hannah, Cheyenne and Charlotte made it special. He'd always be a family with his daughters. Hannah made the picture complete.

As the parade made its way down the street, Noah and Hannah lifted the girls onto their shoulders for a better view. The girls cheered and shouted, clapping their hands in excitement. For a small town, Ramblewood sure didn't skimp on Christmas. The high school marching band was the biggest he'd ever seen. People dressed as reindeer and snowmen handed out candy canes to all the children as they passed by. Parade horses and even some of Clay's alpacas dressed in ugly Christmas sweaters ambled past. Hannah was right, he needed to steer clear of Abby or else he'd be wearing one of those things.

Noah had seen quite a few parades in his day, even marched in some during his time in the air force, but none had compared to this one. He felt as if he'd stepped inside the pages of a storybook. He just hoped it had a happy ending.

WHEN THEY REACHED the firehouse, Charlotte and Cheyenne were barely awake. It was midafternoon and Hannah's plan had been a huge success so far without much effort. Since scaring him off didn't seem likely—not that she truly wanted to anymore—convincing him to move to Ramblewood looked more promising. Noah had repeatedly commented on how much he enjoyed the festival and how they didn't have an event this large in Aurora. Good. One more reason for him to change his mind about trying to take the girls there. Hannah shook the thought from her mind. She didn't want their custody issue to ruin her fun. She needed this break from the drama and so did the girls.

"I almost hate to disturb them." Hannah gazed into the stroller. "But they have to have their picture taken with Santa this year. They were both sick last year, so this will be their first time."

"I'm glad I'm here to share it with them." Noah wrapped his arm around her shoulders and pulled her closer. "And I'm glad I can share it with you."

She rested her head against his shoulder, feeling a sense of peace for the first time in weeks. "You're proving to be a really great father. I'm glad I got to share today with you, too."

"The day isn't over with yet," he whispered against her hair.

"Hello." An elf approached them. "I'm Wendy, Santa's helper. Who do we have here?"

The girls both lifted their heads when they heard Wendy's bell-tipped slippers.

"This is Charlotte and Cheyenne." Hannah rocked the stroller back and forth. She was happy to see they were both extremely interested in Santa's workshop.

"And can I have the last name for the photos?"

"Elgrove."

"Knight."

Hannah barely managed to control her surprise when Noah answered along with her. Wendy tilted her head in confusion.

"The girls' last name is Elgrove." Hannah reiterated, punctuating each letter. *"E-l-g-r-o-v-e."*

Wendy's eyes widened at her tone. She hadn't meant to direct her annoyance at the woman. She hadn't even meant to direct it at Noah. She was stating a fact. Hannah spun to face him. "Please tell me you're not planning to petition the court for a name change."

"My attorney has already done it," he answered.

"What?" She fought to maintain her composure. "You can't take Lauren's last name away from them." She kept her voice low, hoping no one in line behind them would overhear the conversation. "They are her children."

"They are my children, too." He sighed heavily. "If I had been in their lives from the beginning, they would've had my last name."

"I wouldn't bet on that." Hannah's body tensed. "Many unmarried women don't automatically give their children the father's last name. I don't know what Lauren would've done, but I do know they were born with the last name Elgrove and it's going to stay Elgrove."

If she expected a fight from Noah, she didn't get one. He pressed his lips together and looked away. She hated hurting his feelings, but he couldn't just sweep into their lives and change everything. Lauren's death had done a good job of that on its own. She wouldn't let him erase Lauren. Hannah already questioned how much the girls would remember of their mother. They had to at least have her last name.

"Santa will see you now," the elf said cautiously.

Without a word, Noah and Hannah unbuckled the girls from their stroller and sat them on Santa's lap. Charlotte immediately became fascinated with Santa's beard, which thankfully was real or she would've torn it off. Hannah felt bad for Mr. Hanson. He owned and operated the hardware store down the street and had played Santa since she was a kid herself. She wondered how many children tugged at his face over the course of the day. And Cheyenne was just paralyzed, somewhere between shock and amazement.

"Ho ho ho. What would you like Santa to bring you for Christmas?"

"Mommy!" Cheyenne yelled out.

"I want Mommy!" Charlotte followed.

Hannah gripped Noah's arm. She never imagined that the girls would ask Santa for Lauren. Mr. Hanson's eyes met hers.

"Mommy!" Cheyenne wailed louder.

He bounced the girls on his knees in an attempt to soothe them in his best Santa voice, but they continued to call out for Lauren. "No picture is worth this." Hannah took Cheyenne in her arms and wiped her tears. "It's okay, sweetheart."

"Mommy!" she sobbed.

Mr. Hanson stood and handed Charlotte to Noah. "Hannah, I am so sorry."

"It's not your fault." She gave the man a one-armed hug. "Thank you for trying, and thank you for everything you donated to my house. I am forever grateful. Merry Christmas."

They rode back to the ranch in silence. By the time they arrived, the girls were sound asleep. After putting them down for a nap, Hannah slogged to the kitchen and made a pot of coffee. She heard Noah come up behind her, but she didn't have the energy to argue with him any more tonight. He wrapped his arms around her from behind and rested his chin on her shoulder, drawing her close to him.

"I will call my attorney on Monday and ask him not to change the girls' last name."

Hannah sagged against his chest, choking back a sob. "Thank you." Her voice broke.

"When the girls are old enough, we'll let them make the decision."

"We?"

Noah turned her to face him. "Yes, Hannah. We. I can't do this alone. I need you by my side."

Chapter Nine

Noah was determined to salvage what was left of the day. While the children napped, he ventured out to the grocery store. An hour and five bags later, he returned.

"What on earth is all of that?" Hannah peeked inside the sacks.

"You told me I had gingerbread house detail, and I'm reporting for duty." He mock saluted Hannah before giving her a kiss on the cheek. She playfully swatted him out of the way with a kitchen towel. "All of that is for a gingerbread house?"

"Well, I didn't exactly know which recipe to use." Noah rubbed the back of his neck. He didn't even know if the kids were supposed to eat the thing when it was finished or not. "And I wasn't sure which one you would approve of, so I bookmarked a few of them on my phone and bought enough to make all of them just in case something went wrong. I can cook when I choose to, but I can't bake to save my life. Mind if I start on these now?"

"Go right ahead." She smiled. "I'd like the company while I start dinner."

After two burned trays of gingerbread, he finally relented and allowed Hannah to help him. Noah stared down at the table when a successful batch came out of the oven.

"I had grand ambitions when I started this project. Now we're down to four walls and two pieces of roof."

"That's all we're supposed to have, Noah. What were you trying to build? A palace? We have enough stuff to decorate a hundred gingerbread houses."

Noah had wanted to make the girls a gingerbread castle. He doubted Charlotte and Cheyenne had ever had one and he wanted to make them something big and special for his first Christmas with them.

Hannah laughed. "When I put you on gingerbread house duty, I thought you'd pick up a kit with all the stuff in it, not make everything from scratch."

Noah's shoulders dropped. "They make a kit?"

"Yep." Hannah attempted to hide her face behind the dish towel. "It all fits in one shirt-sized box, no baking required."

"Oh, man." Noah flopped onto the chair. "You must think I am the biggest boob."

Hannah braced her hands on his shoulders and leaned over. "No, I think you are the sweetest man to go to this much trouble to make your daughters a gingerbread house. Not many men would do that."

"Speaking of Donner and Blitzen, do you want me to wake them up and get them ready for dinner?"

"If you don't mind. We're running behind schedule tonight. Normally they don't nap this late. We may never get them back to bed later."

Noah didn't think he would ever mind waking up his children. He climbed the stairs to the baby gate. It had taken him a good ten minutes to figure out how to get the thing open earlier. He just hoped Charlotte didn't figure it out anytime soon. Her nimble fingers were able to open anything. He'd be a nervous wreck trying to keep up with her all the time. He came to a sudden stop outside their door. Wasn't that his goal? To take them home and be responsible for them? None of it seemed as easy as he'd originally thought. Hannah needed to come with him and he had to find a way to convince her.

He eased the door open and then remembered they were supposed to pick out new beds for the girls. He didn't want Hannah to have to do it alone, and he wasn't sure if the store would be open in the morning before he flew home. One and a half days with his children was not enough time. Even if he could get beds ordered and delivered, Hannah shouldn't have to contend with taking down the cribs and setting everything up on her own. He didn't know how she managed the kids and her numerous jobs on the ranch. Something had to give before she did. She needed to focus on two things at the most and he knew the only reason she couldn't was because she didn't have the money to hire someone to help her out on the ranch.

Cheyenne sat up, quietly watching him. The second he reached the side of the crib, she raised her arms in the air for him. She didn't vocalize as much as Charlotte, but he'd read that sometimes one twin will talk for the other one.

"Hi there, beautiful." He lowered himself into the glider in the corner of the room, holding her in his arms. He'd seen a lot of this room during his video chats with Hannah. As great as they were, they didn't compare with sitting in the room and being able to touch his children. The sound of Charlotte's deep breathing in the crib and the smell of Cheyenne's hair, which had a piece of candy cane stuck in it, made him never want to leave. It was hard enough going home a week and a half ago. He didn't know how he would do it tomorrow, especially when Christmas was fifteen days away. He'd only get to spend another two and a half days with them between now and then, providing the weather cooperated. He needed more time. They all needed to be in the same state. He'd talk to his real-estate agent on Monday and ask her to expand her search. He'd lost too much time with his kids already.

He wrangled both girls into the bathroom and washed their hands and faces before heading back downstairs. The candy cane chunk in Cheyenne's hair put up a fight, but he eventually got it out.

Hannah served honey mustard–glazed salmon with wild rice and steamed vegetables for dinner. While he was normally a burgers and steak guy, the fresh herbs and homemade glaze had him reaching for seconds. The twins happily munched on their own small pieces with a pureed version of the vegetables.

"This is nice." He reached across the table for Hannah's hand. "The four of us eating dinner together. A man could get very spoiled by this."

"I'm glad you feel that way."

Since Hannah had cooked, Noah insisted on washing the dishes while Hannah cut paper snowflakes and the girls finger-painted cardboard ornaments. Half the kitchen was covered in a plastic drop cloth, and the girls were almost completely covered in paint. The more of a mess they made, the more fun they had.

Noah wasn't a messy guy. He liked things clean, orderly. Chaos drove him crazy, which was probably due to his time in the air force. His helicopters had to be spotless, his clothes wrinkle-free, yet there he was, covered in flour and cinnamon. Both of his daughters had splattered paint on his jeans and he couldn't have been happier. He didn't know when he'd last laughed that hard.

"What we don't use, we can always donate to the food bank you were talking about." Noah sighed. He still needed to go Christmas shopping and then wrap and ship the presents down so they would be ready and waiting when he arrived Christmas weekend. He didn't know what to get the girls. He'd love to buy them an entire toy store, but between the airfare to Texas every weekend, his attorney and the child support on top of his usual expenses, he couldn't afford to go overboard. He made excellent money, but it wasn't that good. Besides, he didn't want Hannah to think he was showing her up by giving them more than she could afford to.

Hannah nodded approvingly. "I think that's a great idea. They ask everyone attending the Mistletoe Rodeo to bring items for the food bank. I'd say we're good to go there."

After Noah figured out how to successfully use a

piping bag, he assembled his little gingerbread house. All that work for something eight inches high. He tore open one of the bags of candy when Hannah stopped him.

"You can't decorate it now. It has to harden overnight or else the weight of the candy will collapse it. We have tomorrow."

"Not really. My flight is at two and we're an hour from the airport. I have to be out of here by noon to allow for traffic and check-in time."

Her mouth dropped open. "They didn't have any later flights?"

"There's one direct flight and it takes five and a half hours. Two thousand miles is a long way from here. I wish I didn't have to go so soon, especially after losing a day to the weather, but hopefully it won't be like this forever." Should he tell her his plan to sell his house and buy a ranch with enough land for her to farm? He wanted to reassure her that he was willing to make the sacrifice in order for them to stay together as a family. But until he had something concrete to show her, he didn't think she'd believe him.

"I want to talk to you about something and I hope I don't offend you." There were too many conversations they needed to have, and if he didn't start having them now, they'd run out of time for those, too.

"Oh, boy." Hannah collapsed into a chair at the table. "Go ahead."

"Well, that's a bit dramatic. This is a good conversation…at least it should be." Noah braced himself for a fight anyway. "The court hasn't determined child support payments yet, but you know they're coming. I'm going to start giving you money weekly now. There's no reason to wait. That being said, I know you're a strong woman and you can do a lot of things, but, Hannah, working at the rodeo school, training and boarding horses, barrel racing on top of trying to run a farm and taking care of the girls is insane. You can't do it all."

Hannah stared down at her hands. "You're not telling me anything I don't already know. But once I'm USDA certified organic, I'll be able to cut back and even hire someone to help me. So thanks, but no thanks. We'll be fine."

"You're not willing to give up anything?"

"If I had to choose, it would be teaching, as much as I love it. The rodeo school is kind of a hassle because it's on the other side of town. I'd hold lessons here, but that requires liability insurance." She held up her hands in defeat. "Boarding horses is a cakewalk compared to everything else, plus it's steady income. The farm isn't too bad, because I'm just managing the soil right now, but I'll be planting my first crops this spring. They won't be classified as organic for another two years, but the land will begin turning a profit. I'm only planting on a handful of acres. Most of my land is horse pasture. So yes, if it came down to it, I guess I could give up the farm, because I have to keep putting money into it before I'll see any return on my investment. I don't want to, though. And I can't possibly give up barrel racing. That's who I am. That would be like you giving up being a pilot. All that leaves is training horses and there's no overhead involved there."

"Could you afford to hire someone to help you run the farm now or even in the spring?"

"Not until it's generating revenue." Hannah pushed away from the table and grabbed a bottle of wine from the fridge. She uncorked it and poured them each a glass. "I know I have to give up something. I just haven't figured out what yet. It's not an easy decision. I have to think long-term."

Hannah's acknowledgment of the problem was a start. Moving to Oregon would be the best solution, but without anything solid to offer her, it was nothing more than a thought. Heavy conversations were not the way he wanted to spend his Saturday night.

"I know we haven't talked about it today." She tilted her head toward the girls. "I think now would be the perfect time to tell them who you are."

The thought had been at the back of his mind since he'd landed. He'd hoped to discuss it after the parade, but then the Santa incident happened and he'd decided they'd had enough for one day.

"Are you sure? You were against it last week."

"It's been weighing on me for days. The big difference between now and the last time we discussed it is your communication with them. We hadn't established a nightly routine yet. I think they need to know they have one parent." Hannah stood and grabbed a few clean dish towels from the drawer. "I'm Aunt Hannah. I'm not mom and I'm not dad. They need a dad. They need you. After what I saw today, I've never been surer of it."

Noah washed his hands and scrubbed his face in the kitchen sink before sitting down across from Charlotte and Cheyenne at the table. No matter how much he'd practiced this moment, he'd forgotten everything he wanted to say.

"Hey, you two." Noah looked to Hannah for help. "I don't know how to begin."

"Charlotte, Cheyenne, can you two look at me for a minute?" The girls looked up, big blue eyes in a sea of multicolored paint. "You know how Grandpop is my daddy?"

Charlotte plopped a painted hand on her sister's head and laughed. Cheyenne returned the favor to the side of the face.

"I think we're losing our audience." Noah laughed.

"Play nice, girls." Hannah leaned across the table and wiped the paint out of Charlotte's nose.

"Are you sure that stuff washes off?"

Cheyenne attempted to protect her sister and tried to wrestle the towel away from Hannah. "I've been making this for them since they were a year old. It's only water and flour with some gel food coloring. I make another type of paint for the bathtub. They love it." Hannah let Cheyenne have the towel. She then proceeded to clean her sister with it. "Girls, how would you like to have a daddy to love and to love you back?" Charlotte began clapping and Cheyenne stilled. "You would like that, wouldn't you?" Hannah reached across the table and lightly tickled both of their bellies before looking at Noah. "There is your cue."

Noah moved his chair closer to their high chairs. "How would you like it if I was your daddy?" he asked.

"Okay," Charlotte said and then went back to her finger painting.

Cheyenne reached for his hand and pulled him toward her.

"What about you, sweetheart? Do you want me to be your daddy?"

"Love you," she shouted and then began banging her palms on her high chair tray.

Any chance of not shedding a tear ended there. His chest swelled. His heart was about to burst through his shirt. "I love you, too, Cheyenne. You have no idea how much." He lifted her out of her chair and hugged her tight. Her little hands twisted in his hair as she babbled against his neck. Tears clouded his eyes, choking his voice. "I'll be yours forever."

AFTER A BATH and a clean set of clothes all around, they all piled on the couch and watched *A Charlie Brown Christmas* and *Santa Claus is Comin' to Town*. The girls sat between them, giggling and happy. Hannah had almost forgotten she and Noah were battling each other for custody. They felt like a family. And she liked it. Too much, because regardless of Noah telling her he wanted to give their relationship a chance, they needed to be together—every day, not just weekends—for it to work. She was running out of time before he left in the morning.

Hannah gathered everyone's clothes and tossed them in the washing machine, giving Noah a chance to read a bedtime story to his daughters alone. She hadn't been sure how they would react to the news, and she still wasn't sure how much they understood. At least they had someone to call Daddy, and however Noah had come into their lives, she couldn't imagine any other man as their father.

The moment, as beautiful as it had been, was bittersweet. The closer Noah became to his daughters, the further she felt them slipping away. She wanted to trust him. She wanted to believe he would never cut her out of their lives, but once their birth certificate was changed and a court gave him parental rights, she wouldn't be their guardian any longer. She'd have no ties to them whatsoever. At least not legally. He could take them and move to another country and she would be powerless to stop him.

An echo of laughter traveled through the house. The children were happy and that was what mattered most, right? Not her feelings. She didn't want to be selfish. But dammit, she'd helped raise those children just as much as a father would have.

"Hannah." She jumped at the sound of his voice.

"You scared me half to death." She hadn't heard him come in over the sound of the dryer. "Are the girls asleep already?" She hated the thought of not tucking them in. She wasn't ready to give that up.

"They're getting there. They want you to read them a story now."

"I knew their afternoon nap would throw their little sleep cycles off."

Hannah was surprised when Noah followed her upstairs. She'd hoped to have a few minutes alone with the girls, for no other reason than it had been a long day and she wanted to make sure they were okay. Their reactions were harder to read when he was around. They fixated on him because he was shiny and new. And that was great. She wanted them to love him. But it hurt at the same time.

"How about we read *Goodnight Moon*?" It had been one of their favorites and their eyes were so heavy with sleep, she didn't think they'd last through the first couple pages. A few minutes later, they were both out. She used to love watching them fall asleep before Lauren had moved to Boston. She still loved it.

Noah cleared his throat from the doorway. She didn't know if he wanted her attention or if it had been more of a cough. She closed her eyes, laid her head against the back of the glider and ignored him. This was her moment and the rest of the world could wait.

Hannah remained upstairs until she heard the sound of popcorn popping away. It must have been one more thing Noah had bought at the store. When she came downstairs, she was surprised at the amount of popcorn he'd made. He appeared to have filled every one of her bowls and a stockpot.

"Making a little snack?" she asked.

Noah handed her two bowls and motioned for her to follow him. "I don't have much time to help you get ready for Christmas, so tonight you and I are stringing popcorn." He led her into the living room and sat on the floor next to the bowls he'd already set out. "I even picked up needles and thread. I figured it was easier to do this one without the girls. I hope you don't mind that I searched your cabinets for a hot air popper.

I was fully prepared to make it on the stove top if you didn't have one."

"No, I don't mind." Hannah joined him on the floor. "I haven't done this since I was a kid. You know, you don't have to jam everything into one day. We still have next weekend."

"It's not enough time." He handed her a spool of thread. "Plus, we need to go to the furniture store and look at beds. Are they open tomorrow?"

"No, not much is open around here on Sunday."

"Crap. Let me get my checkbook." He started to get up when Hannah reached out.

"Noah, stop."

"I told you I would pay for the beds." He twisted out of her grasp. "Make sure you tell them to deliver them and set them up, too. You shouldn't be doing all that, and if I can't be here, then I'll pay someone to do it. If I don't give you enough, have them call me and I'll put the rest on a credit card."

"Noah," she said louder, hoping she hadn't woken the girls. "You can give me the check later. Even if we had picked out the beds today, I would have had to wait for them to be delivered. They never have that stuff in stock. They may not even come until after the holidays. You're not missing anything there."

"That's true." Noah settled back down beside her and opened the pack of needles.

"You won't be missing anything during the week, either." She began stringing the popcorn. "I have a lot to do here, plus Christmas shopping and—" Hannah took a deep breath and steadied herself "—Lauren's things arrived from Boston last week. Her entire apartment. The company she worked for had everything packed and shipped down, including the furniture, which I hadn't expected. It's all stored in my parents' barn, but I need to go through it."

"Why didn't you tell me?" He leaned closer and laid his arm around her shoulders, wrapping her in a blanket of comfort.

"I didn't want to think about it until after the holidays."

"Then why are you going through the boxes next week?"

"Because Lauren always did everything months in advance." Hannah attempted a smile. "I'm willing to bet there are Christmas presents for the girls in those boxes. I can't leave gifts in the barn knowing Lauren took such great care picking them out for her daughters. Maybe she hadn't had an opportunity to shop yet with the new job and new place, but I'm not willing to take that chance. The girls deserve one last present from their mom, and if they're in there, I will find them."

"I wish I could be here to help you."

"Thank you." Hannah tugged a bowl of popcorn closer to her. "This is something I need to do on my own." She nodded to his lowly strand of garland. "You're falling way behind."

He tossed a piece of popcorn at her. "Can I ask you something?"

"I think you just did." She tossed one back.

"Do you want to have your own biological children one day?"

She hadn't expected that question. "If you had been around during Lauren's pregnancy, you wouldn't ask that."

"Why?"

"She had an extremely difficult time." Hannah winced at the recollection. "She wasn't just carrying twins. They were very large twins. And they wanted to eat, all the time. She had the worst cravings for the most god-awful combinations you can imagine. Everything from sardine-flavored shakes to peanut butter meat loaf."

"That's horrible." Noah's face contorted in disgust.

"Imagine being the one having to make the sardine shakes. And then I had to watch her consume them." Hannah had become very well acquainted with her gag reflex during those nine months. "Lauren had morning sickness from the beginning until the middle of her seventh month."

"Are you sure it was morning sickness and not a reaction to whatever it was she was eating?" Noah frowned.

"I know, right? Lauren and I had had that same argument many times. She was only five foot two. So the bigger those babies grew, the more uncomfortable she became. Think about a normal pregnancy. A woman her size carrying around a seven-pound baby plus the extra goodies that come with it. She was caring around twice that. She had a hard time sleeping and working. The doctor put her on bed rest at eight months. The restriction drove her insane. And the delivery… Oh, my God."

"Did she have a cesarean?"

"Nope." Hannah shook her head. "She delivered naturally. Sixteen hours of labor. After witnessing her ordeal, I don't have a strong desire to give birth. Besides, I feel as if Charlotte and Cheyenne are half mine. I essentially became the other parent."

Noah's eyes shifted to the floor. "I hadn't looked at it that way."

"Now maybe you'll understand why they mean so much to me." She searched his face for some sign he'd stay in Ramblewood with the girls, but he was unreadable. She had a few more hours in the morning to convince him, and she knew the perfect place to go. A place everyone was welcome and Lauren's girls were cherished. She'd take him to church.

Chapter Ten

When Hannah said she had somewhere special to take him, Noah never anticipated it would be the Ramble-wood Community Church. Not that he minded.

The historic white chapel was beautifully simple with its open rafter interior, white walls and hand-hewn pine pews. A Christmas tree made from red poinsettia plants filled one of the back corners, a large hand-carved nativity scene in the other. Candles and pine boughs adorned the modest altar while sunlight filtered through the tall divided windows, illuminating the entire service.

Noah came from a town with a population of less than one thousand. He understood small-town life. But he'd never seen people welcome a stranger as graciously as he'd been welcomed. Just about everybody there had already known who he was before they were introduced. He recognized some faces from the volunteers who had come out to work on Hannah's house. Others he remembered from his first morning in town. And then there were a slew of people he'd never laid eyes on who called him by name.

They sat with Hannah's family while Charlotte and Cheyenne played in the nursery with their friends. Noah was surprised at how many friends two almost twenty-two-month-old children had. He hadn't had the opportunity to see his daughters interact with other children before. They happily played, hardly noticing when he and Hannah left them to attend the service.

"It was nice to see you in attendance this morning, Noah." The pastor firmly shook his hand as they exited the church. "I do hope you'll be joining us for lunch in the fellowship hall."

Noah checked his watch. It was quarter after eleven and he needed to be on the road no later than noon. "I can stay for fifteen minutes at the most, but I have a plane to catch."

"I wish you could stay longer." Hannah's mother joined their conversation. "Hannah and the girls both miss you when you're gone."

"I miss them, too," he said. "I can only get away for three and a half days every week and a good portion of that time is spent getting to Ramblewood."

"Maybe you should move here."

Well, that was blunt. Noah wished it were that easy. "My job is highly specialized and they don't have heli-loggers around here."

Fern laughed. "No, but we do have helicopters."

"True, but it's not the same. I'm not just a helicopter pilot."

The pastor motioned for them to move their conversation farther down the stairs so they weren't blocking the doorway.

"Would it be so bad if you were?" Fern asked. "Look, Noah. I like you. I didn't at first, but you've grown on me and you've grown on my daughter. Having kids means sometimes making sacrifices. The kids have a good life here. Please consider that before you decide to take them away from all of this."

Noah's jaw clenched. He'd basically asked Hannah to do the same thing last night. "There you are." Hannah's fingers lightly grazed his arm. "It's time to get the girls from the nursery. They were just invited to a play date this week by a mom with another set of twins. I promise I'll take lots of pictures and send them to you."

Noah rubbed his temples. "Hannah, I'm afraid I have to pass on lunch. It's getting too late and I can't afford to miss my flight."

The happiness slid from her face. "Okay."

"I'm sorry." Noah hated tearing her and the children away from her family and friends. "Why don't you stay here and enjoy the afternoon? I'll reinstall the car seats in your truck, and if you give me your key so I can get in, I'll lock up the house and leave the key wherever you want."

Hannah hesitated before agreeing. "This is the first time we've been back to church since Lauren died." She reached into her bag and removed her house keys. "It's the first time the girls have been here since they moved to Boston." She fumbled with the fob, dropping it before managing to remove the house key. "It will be good for them to spend the rest of the day with their little playmates. I really wish you could stay."

Me, too. "Let's go pick up the girls so I can say

goodbye." Noah swallowed hard. "I'll be back before you know it."

"Yeah." Hannah kept her head down and walked slightly in front of him. He hated disappointing her, even though she'd known he was leaving.

If he thought saying goodbye to Hannah was difficult, it didn't compare to saying goodbye to his daughters. He didn't know how much more he could take of this arrangement. He had to bring Hannah and the girls home before he found it impossible to say goodbye. Despite Fern's suggestion, moving to Ramblewood wasn't an option for him. He'd be insane to give up years of training and his salary when there was a more practical solution.

Noah was miserable by the time he arrived home. Unlocking the door, he stepped inside, greeted by emptiness. No laughter, not a single Christmas decoration, no Hannah, no girls. He sent a quick text message saying he was home and promising to call later. He knew the girls were already in bed and he was in too foul a mood to talk now. He fired off another message to his real-estate agent asking her to expand her search. He'd follow it up tomorrow with a telephone call, because he needed to feel like he was doing something about the situation. Even his attorney had agreed he had to move sooner than later. Without a home inspection, they couldn't determine custody. Noah didn't want to risk losing custody of his own children because of where he lived. So they were at a standstill until he found a new house.

HANNAH WANTED TO COLLAPSE. Cheyenne had the flu and it was only a matter of time before Charlotte came down with it, too. She hadn't had a decent night's sleep in the two days since Noah left and a raging headache was making her left eye twitch. The strong, single-mom thing was all well and good, but when there was a dad available, she believed in equal time in sickness and in health. If Noah were there, she was certain he'd help her. Heck, he told her as much every time he called, but it wasn't the same as actually being there.

Her mom and Abby had offered to help, but she couldn't risk their health. She had no choice but to do it alone. Clay stopped by twice a day to tend to the horses for her, but her teaching, training and practice schedules had come to a screeching halt.

The video chat chimed on her phone. She accepted the call wordlessly.

"Oh, honey, that's not a good look for you." Noah's face filled the screen, brows furrowed. "How are you doing tonight or shouldn't I ask?"

"How come you get the happy Charlotte and Cheyenne and I get the pukey ones?"

"Well, that answers my next question. I guess Cheyenne hasn't improved this afternoon. Is your eye twitching or is it the connection?"

"No, it's me, and no, she hasn't improved. The doctor said the meds usually take three days. So here's hoping tomorrow will be the day."

"I'm sorry you have to do this alone."

Hannah had dealt with sick kids before, but she would take turns with Lauren caring for them. This was the first time she had to truly handle everything by herself and it was terrifying. Especially in the middle of the night when one of them spiked a fever.

"Would it be selfish of me to say I wish you were here?" Hannah asked.

"Not at all." He smiled. "I miss you. Not just the girls, I miss you, too."

"Even my toes?" Noah's calls had been the one bright spot in her otherwise dreary days. Unfortunately, every time he had called, Cheyenne was asleep. Between the flu and the medicine, she slept most of the day, while Charlotte was a bundle of energy. Once midnight rolled around, Charlotte was out cold and Cheyenne kept Hannah awake most of the night.

"Even your toes. I take it the girls are in bed." Noah's expectant face almost broke her heart.

"I'm sorry." Hannah yawned. "They went down a half hour ago. I think it's the first time they've both been asleep at the same time since Sunday. They were cranky when they were awake. Be glad you missed it."

"I'd rather not miss any of it." Noah disappeared from the screen for a few seconds before reappearing, his eyes glassy. "As much as I would love to talk to you, why don't you try to get some sleep? At least until they get up again."

"Okay." Hannah ran her fingers across the screen, wishing she could touch his face or kiss him good-night. "I'll call you if anything changes."

Noah nodded. "Hannah, I—um… I—I'll talk to you soon."

"Good night." She disconnected the call, wondering

what Noah wanted to say but hadn't. He couldn't possibly have been about to say I love you, could he? Nah. Hannah checked all the doors and climbed the stairs to bed after checking in on the girls one last time. She crawled between the sheets, wishing Noah were there to hold her close. Maybe someday they'd have that chance.

BY THURSDAY MORNING, Cheyenne was feeling better, but Charlotte had come down with the flu. Noah had caught a flight late last night and was due to arrive any minute. As much as she wanted to see him, as soon as he walked through that door, he was on kid duty.

She had to get some rest before Saturday's Mistletoe Rodeo. She'd made a commitment and intended to see it through. She hoped Noah could handle playing nursemaid. If he was determined to take the girls to Oregon, he needed to see how tough it was looking after a sick kid. So far, all he'd had was the happy, healthy twin experience.

Hannah heard his rental truck pull into the drive. Her butt was firmly planted on the couch and she didn't have the energy to get up and greet him at the door. She'd unlocked it when she came down the stairs and was sure he'd figure it out.

"Hey, sweetheart. Aren't you feeling well?" Noah dropped his bag in the foyer and sat beside her on the couch. She could only imagine what she looked like. Sweatpants, T-shirt, robe, ponytail. After cleaning up barf, she wasn't in the mood to do her hair and apply a slick of lipstick. Noah needed a good dose of reality.

She rested her head on his shoulder and allowed him

to envelop her in his arms. Their strength felt more incredible than she had imagined. Hannah had never been a "curl up on the couch and snuggle" kind of girl…until now. She could easily lay her head on his chest and listen to his heartbeat until she fell asleep. "Thank you for coming early. I hope it didn't mess up your job."

"My boss wasn't happy, but he understood." Noah smoothed her hair. "What can I do to help you?"

Hannah sat upright, instantly missing the comfort of his embrace. For a man who had worked all day and then flown all night, he seemed remarkably awake in his black chamois shirt and dark jeans. With the exception of one errant lock of blond hair that had fallen across his forehead, he looked perfect.

She pushed off the couch and stood. "I know you've had a long flight, but I would really appreciate a few hours of sleep. Can you please take care of the twins for a little while?"

"Of course." Noah helped her to her room and gave her a chaste kiss at the door. Well, a peck on the top of the head. She wouldn't want to kiss her when she looked like this, either. "I have a baby monitor in my room, so just holler if you need me. The thermometer is on the dresser in their room. You stick it in her ear, press the button, and it almost instantly tells you her temperature. If you can't figure it out, wake me. Actually, wake me if you need anything at all. I gave Charlotte her medicine two hours ago, so she'll probably sleep well for now. Hopefully." Hannah turned to walk into her bedroom and stopped. "Thank you and welcome home."

She closed the door behind herself and collapsed on the bed. Finally.

No sooner had she closed her eyes, she heard a knock at the door. "What?"

"Hannah?" Noah opened the door and stuck his head in, the light from the hallway blinding her. "Charlotte just threw up."

Hannah sighed. "Clean up what you can of it, throw it in the garbage, put her in clean pajamas, check her diaper because usually when she does one she does the other, change the bedding and throw everything in the washing machine after you take her temperature. Do you want me to come show you?"

"Um, no. I got it. Go back to sleep." He eased the door closed.

Hannah knew she'd have to get up and help him, but she wanted to see how far he'd make it on his own. She rolled over and grabbed the baby monitor from the nightstand. She squinted as he appeared on screen. "Is he wearing my latex gloves from under the bathroom sink?" Hannah shook her head. He held Charlotte as far away from his body as possible while still maintaining a hold on her. Hannah laughed. The man had completed four tours of duty in Iraq, had one of the world's most dangerous jobs, and he was afraid of a little toddler vomit. "He'll learn."

After successfully changing Charlotte into clean clothes, he took her temperature. "100.6," he announced. She didn't know if he said it aloud for his benefit or hers, but she was thankful he did. It wasn't high enough for her to be overly concerned, but she knew another trip to the

pediatrician was on her agenda tomorrow. Correction…
on both of their agendas.

Noah stayed with Charlotte until she fell back to
sleep, then he disappeared from the screen. She heard
the stairs creak and assumed he was on his way to do
the laundry. When he returned a few minutes later, she
fully expected him to check on the twins and head back
downstairs to watch television. Instead, he propped his
feet up on the ottoman and fell asleep in the glider. She
had to give him credit. She hadn't thought he had it in
him. Confident he had everything under control, Hannah pulled the covers around herself and went to sleep.

NOAH AWOKE WITH a stiff neck and back. Easing out of
the chair, he checked on the twins. He'd spent the last
twenty hours cleaning up one toddler explosion after
another. Relieved to see them both still asleep, he sat
back down, wiped out after just one night. He couldn't
imagine the four days Hannah had dealt with. No wonder she'd craved sleep so desperately yesterday. Noah
sneaked into the hall, careful not to wake her as he
passed her door. He didn't know what time it was. He
tiptoed downstairs to make a pot of coffee when he
noticed one was already made. Hannah was awake?
He checked the clock on the wall. Six a.m. Of course
she was. She'd probably mucked the stalls, cleaned the
henhouse, exercised the horses and run a marathon by
now. She did more before sunrise than he ever had in
the service. At least she'd gotten a good night's sleep,
which was more than he could say. It was only fair, but
it wasn't the night he had planned during his flight back

to Oregon last week. He had hoped for a romantic evening. A fire, a glass of wine, a movie on TV. It didn't
need to be anything epic, he just wanted some alone
time with Hannah. Everything they did revolved around
the kids, and while that had been great, he wanted some
downtime with just her.

"Good morning," Hannah said from the mudroom
doorway. "How did you sleep?" Her lips curled upward
devilishly.

"I think I've mastered your washing machine."

"That good, huh?" Hannah frowned. "How many
more times?"

"A few." Noah filled two cups of coffee. "What happens now? Does she need to go back to the doctor?"

"I've already left a message with the pediatrician's
answering service. They will call when they get in and
hopefully we'll get an appointment today. I thought it
was the same thing Cheyenne had, but she didn't throw
up this much. When in doubt, call the doctor." She sat
her coffee mug down. "Depending on when the appointment is, I may have to meet you there. I'll give
you directions."

"You're leaving?" Noah wasn't sure he liked that
idea.

"I've missed the last three days of work and I need
to meet my students at the rodeo school for one final
practice before they compete tomorrow. I have to finish my Christmas shopping at some point today, too.
You don't mind, do you?"

That meant even less time that Noah would have
to spend with Hannah. "No, I told you all week that I

wished I had been here to help you, and here I am. I can handle a sick child. I may not know what to do, but I'm willing to learn."

He hated that Hannah had to go through so much of this alone. It was bad enough she still had Lauren's belongings to contend with. She hadn't told him much last week except she'd found a few shopping bags containing unwrapped toys and had assumed Lauren bought them for Christmas. Hannah had wrapped them, put Lauren's name on them and set them under the tree, but when they spoke Wednesday morning, she still hadn't decided when to give them to the girls. She was afraid it would ruin their Christmas.

"I appreciate it. You should get to know their doctor and I'm sure you probably have questions as a first-time dad." Hannah crossed the kitchen, opened the pantry door and removed a key hanging from a nail. "This is for you." She handed it to him. "I'm trusting you. I've never given anyone a key to my house with the exception of my family and Lauren. Everything's going to be really crazy between now and Christmas, and in case I'm not here, you can get in."

"Thank you."

"Well, I have to get back to work. I saw the light on in the kitchen and thought I should come in and say good morning."

"Good morning."

Hannah's face brightened for the first time since he'd arrived. It bothered him that this week had been so hard on her. At twenty-four, she should be out having a good time with her friends, not stuck at home with him and two toddlers. Either she was great at covering the letdown or she was even stronger than he'd originally thought. Out of all the women in the world, Noah was thankful Hannah was his partner in raising the children. He hoped one day soon that they could be much more.

HANNAH WAS EXHAUSTED when she arrived home from the rodeo school. Noah had called and texted her a few times with updates on the girls. Cheyenne seemed to be holding steady and Charlotte had thrown up only once since they left the pediatrician's office. It was a bug going around that they'd probably caught at church. Typical kid sickness. Noah had handled it better than she'd hoped.

She pulled around to the back of the house and fed the horses. She checked the henhouse, but Noah had already collected the eggs. She was grateful for any help he offered. When she stepped in the mudroom, the incredible aroma of pasta sauce made her stomach growl instantly.

"Oh, my God, that smells so good." Hannah slipped off her boots and lifted the pot lid. "This doesn't look like it came from a jar. Did you make this from scratch?"

"I told you I could cook. I just tend not to when it's only me." Noah gave his sauce a stir. "We're having grilled chicken breast and whole wheat pasta topped with my famous sauce and a side of broccoli for dinner. I hope that's okay."

His voice had already begun to lull her into a better mood. "It's more than okay." He had set the table with the red tablecloth she had stashed in the pantry and had even placed a Christmas-scented jar candle she'd had in another room in the center of the table. He definitely had romance in mind. Hannah thought it was sweet. No one had ever done that for her before.

"Are the girls already in bed?"

"Charlotte could barely keep her eyes open after her last dose of medicine and Cheyenne was beat from trying to wear me out. They made a valiant effort to stay awake for you, but sleep won out."

"My poor babies. I'll check in on them. I'm going to go shower and change because I'm really horsey right now. I'll be back down in fifteen minutes. And, Noah, thank you."

HANNAH WAS SO FULL after dinner she could've rolled into the living room. Noah had made a fatal mistake tonight. By letting her know he could cook that well, she now expected him to do so more often.

"How would you like to watch Christmas movies tonight?" Noah asked.

"I'd love to, but I think there are only children's movies on. I don't get many channels."

He reached under the couch and removed two DVDs. "That's why I came prepared."

Hannah couldn't believe he stashed movies under her couch. "What else do you have under there?"

"You never know." He leaned closer to her. "I'm full of surprises." He took her face in his hands and held it gently. Her skin prickled in anticipation as his mouth covered hers, slow and intoxicating. She buried her hands deep in his hair, urging him closer. "I'd love to come home to this every night," she said against his lips.

"Sweetheart, I was just thinking the same thing." He kissed her once more before easing from her grasp. "If I don't put this in now, we will never see these movies."

Hannah couldn't remember how much of the movies they actually watched. Somewhere between the first and millionth kiss, she gave a part of her heart to Noah.

Chapter Eleven

"Get out." Fern Tanner startled Noah as she stormed into the kitchen.

He backed away from the children's high chairs and into the counter. "Excuse me?" Noah quickly tried to run through what he could've done to upset the woman.

"My daughter is on the way to the Mistletoe Rodeo pancake brunch and you're going to meet her there."

Noah let out a sigh of relief. "I know she is, and I told her I would stay home with the girls." He finished wiping off Cheyenne's face. "Cheyenne's feeling better, but Charlotte still won't eat, which may be a good thing after last night."

"That's why I'm here." Fern felt Charlotte's cheeks with the back of her hand. "She's a little warm. What's her temperature?"

"It's 99.2 and no." Noah shook his head. "Hannah would kill me if I left them with you. She feels—and I agree—that you've already done enough. We don't want you to get what they have."

"Nonsense. Gage and I have both had our flu shots." She squeezed between him and the girls. "I've had decades more experience with sick children than the two of you, so if I say you're going to brunch with my daughter, you're going."

Noah folded his arms. "The first week I was here I wondered if you were playing matchmaker. Now I'm convinced."

"I'm not playing matchmaker." Fern feigned innocence. "I'm a firm believer that everything happens for a reason. What happened to Lauren was tragic and I would do anything to bring her back. But there was a reason you found my daughter. That obituary happened to be in the right place at the right time. Maybe it was a sign from above or even Lauren herself. I believe you and Hannah are meant to be together. I would love to see something good come from this tragedy. I think it's wonderful that the girls have you for a father, but I feel there's something bigger there."

Noah debated how much to tell Fern about his relationship with her daughter. He was surprised she didn't know they were... They were what? They hadn't even figured it out yet. No wonder Hannah had kept quiet.

"I probably shouldn't be telling you this, but Hannah and I have discussed it."

Fern's expression sprang to life.

"Don't get too excited. We're taking things one day at a time. It's hard living in two separate states."

"Then maybe you should live in the same state. You're already living together."

"We're—we're not— It's not like that. I have my own room." He did not want to have this conversation with Hannah's mother. "We're working on the same state thing."

Fern clapped her hands together in excitement. "You are! That's wonderful, Noah."

He had a feeling—a very strong feeling—that Fern assumed he meant he was moving to Texas and he didn't have the heart to correct her. If she truly felt Hannah and he belonged together, then she would accept their living in Oregon. He hoped, anyway, considering his real-estate agent had shown him a couple of properties that had potential. They were great, but still not quite right. She'd had one more property on her list, but it had a sale pending. When she'd heard the potential buyers were having difficulty securing a mortgage, Noah had gone to see the place just in case the deal fell through. It was perfect. It was the ideal ranch for Hannah, with plenty of room for farming.

"I don't exactly have the details worked out yet." That was the truth.

"Answer me one question." Fern urged him to sit. "Are you genuinely interested in pursuing a relationship with Hannah? Or do you only want to be with her because of the girls?"

Noah attempted to reassure her. "My family is not complete without Hannah. And it's not complete without Charlotte and Cheyenne. I don't know how to love one without the other. They're a package deal to me."

Fern gasped. "Are you telling me you're in love with my Hannah?"

Noah wasn't sure who was more surprised by his declaration, Fern or him. He could no longer imagine a future without the four of them together. But love? Warning bells sounded in his head. "You're really putting me on the spot. *Love* is a very strong word with many different definitions."

Fern grabbed his cheeks and kissed him on the forehead. "Then I suggest you go find my daughter and figure it out. And I don't want to see you back here anytime soon. There are many events going on today besides the rodeo. Take her out somewhere tonight. I will take care of the kids. Don't worry about a thing. If Charlotte gets worse, I'll call you, but I'm sure we'll have it under control. Gage will stop by later. Go and have a good time. You two deserve some fun."

"Thank you." Noah gave her a hug before kissing his daughters. He bounded upstairs to grab his wallet and phone, excited about having a day alone with Hannah. Well, as alone as he could get in the middle of a rodeo, but he'd take it.

Was Fern right? Was he in love with Hannah? He knew his feelings for her were intensifying, but love?

Does she love me? Noah didn't know which thought terrified him more…loving Hannah or Hannah loving him. Either way, he'd never felt more alive.

NOAH SCANNED THE crowd at the church fellowship hall for Hannah. The scent of fresh pancakes and maple syrup cruelly taunted him. He'd already eaten breakfast, but he was positive he'd find room for another one. Spotting her in the far corner, he crossed the room to her table as half the town greeted him along the way.

"Noah!" Hannah jumped to her feet, almost knocking over her chair. "Why are you here, is something wrong with the girls?"

Noah placed his hands on her shoulders to calm her. "The girls are fine. Your mom came over and told me to get out. Actually said the words *get out*."

Clay began laughing. "Yep, that sounds like Mom."

"She told me to find you and make sure we have fun today," Noah continued. "And she stressed that we're not to come back anytime soon and not to worry about her and your father because they've already had their flu shots."

Abby covered her mouth, laughing. "Fern really covered her bases, didn't she?"

Hannah sagged against him. "You really scared me for a moment." She moved over so he could take a seat at the table. "In the future all you have to say is *Fern* and we'll understand." Everyone laughed. She passed Noah the platter of pancakes and a jug of syrup. "This is an all-you-can-eat thing, but a word of warning, it will sneak up on you. You tend to realize you've had too much five pancakes too late."

"Where are you off to after this?" Noah asked as he happily ate his second breakfast for the day.

"I have to head over to the arena. My girls are allowed to get in some practice time before the show."

"You're more than welcome to join us," Abby said.

Clay nudged her. "I think the whole idea of my mom kicking him out was so that they would spend time together, not with us."

Abby shrugged. "Well, if you change your mind, we'll be around."

"You're more than welcome to come with me to the arena. Maybe if you saw my little barrel racers, you wouldn't be as worried about Charlotte and Cheyenne on a horse."

He doubted he'd ever get used to the idea of his beautiful children on top of a half-ton animal. "Sounds like a plan."

It didn't take Noah long to understand what Hannah had meant about the pancakes. After brunch, he followed her to the arena and walked around the exterior stands twice before he felt like he wouldn't explode from all the food he'd eaten. Then he watched from the stands as the girls practiced, almost dying from the adorableness of the three-year-old barrel racer on a miniature pony. If that was what his daughters would be doing, maybe the sport wasn't so bad after all. Hannah came in second place during her event, and Noah suspected she may have lost on purpose to a woman overwhelmed with joy for the saddle she'd just won.

Between the rodeo clowns and ostrich races, Noah once again found himself laughing hysterically in Hannah's presence. The rodeo scene had never grown on him. But whenever he was out with Hannah and her family, he had an amazing time. Maybe there was something to the lifestyle. It made him even more excited at the prospect of buying the ranch in Oregon.

After checking in on the twins repeatedly during the day, he felt relaxed enough to take Fern's advice and treat Hannah to dinner.

"I saw a little honky-tonk joint the first night I was

in town. Do you want to go there, get something to eat and take a spin on the dance floor?"

"Slater's Mill? That's definitely not the place to go unless you want an audience. Not only do my brother and Abby go there almost every night, so do the rest of my friends."

"Then you tell me where."

"Do you like chocolate?"

"How could anyone not like chocolate?" Noah asked.

"There's a place on Main Street called Le Chocolat that serves chocolate fondue with probably a hundred different types of food to dip in it. I went there once for my birthday, and I've been dying to go back there again."

"Show me the way." French, romantic, chocolate, Hannah. Yeah, that was exactly the kind of evening Noah had in mind.

When they arrived, the dimly lit restaurant was cozier than he had expected. The building was very narrow and long, and instead of tables, everyone had a curved booth. Good for cuddling up to your date. He was glad when Hannah scooted all the way to the middle, her thigh lightly pressed against his. The heat from her body alone would have melted the chocolate.

"You weren't kidding when you said there were over a hundred items to choose from." They decided on the three-chocolate sampler: milk, dark and Chilean with a twenty-item dipper and a zinfandel to share.

Once the waiter took their order and left their table, Noah gently hooked her chin and turned her to face him. She lifted her mouth and brushed a gentle kiss across his lips. He slipped his arm around her waist, pulling her closer. Reclaiming her lips, his kiss was slow and demanding. She freely gave herself to him as her tongue caressed his, sending shivers down his spine. Noah broke their kiss and stared into her eyes. A slow, easy smile spread across her face as she looked up at him. He couldn't imagine being anywhere else, with anyone else. Maybe this was what love felt like.

HANNAH DIDN'T KNOW anything about aphrodisiacs, but she would swear everything they had just eaten classified as one. Her body tingled and ached for Noah's touch. She didn't want to go home. She wanted to go somewhere secluded where she could spend the night in his arms. They had options on the highway, but she'd rather their first time together happened in a honeymoon hotel rather than an hourly one. Resisting the urge to explore his body further, she opted for a moonlit walk around Ramblewood Park's animated light display.

Noah entwined his fingers with hers and she reveled in the possessive way he claimed her hand. He made her feel special and wanted. And she wanted him in more ways than just sexually. She almost couldn't bear the thought of him leaving tomorrow. The separation, even if only for four days, was almost intolerable, especially in the middle of the night when all she wanted to do was roll over and lay her head against his chest and listen to the sound of his heartbeat. She wanted his heart to beat for her, for their family. She wanted him to stay.

As they walked through a tunnel of red-and-white

twinkling candy canes, Noah stopped and twirled her into his arms.

She giggled against him. "What was that for?"

"I want to be able to tell the girls someday that I danced with you under candy cane stars." He slid his hands into her back pockets and began swaying to the Christmas music that played throughout the park. "I wish we could do this every night."

"I wish we could, too." She snuggled closer to him.

"Do you really mean that? Can you really see yourself spending every night with me?"

Hannah gazed up at him. "Noah, I couldn't imagine myself with anybody else."

"You know," Noah said. He slowly slid his hand out of her pocket and up her waist, lingering over her ribs until he grazed the underside of her breast. She inhaled sharply, then checked over her shoulder to make sure nobody was watching. "If you and I made this permanent, then we wouldn't have to worry about custody agreements or court."

"Are you—" Her voice stuck in her throat. "Are you trying to seduce me into agreeing to a relationship?" As much as she wanted him, a part of her still felt she was betraying her best friend.

"I'm trying to seduce you into agreeing to much more than a relationship." He placed a featherlight kiss upon her lips. "I'm thinking more of a commitment to each other and our family. I don't want you to say yes just yet, but I do want you to think about it."

If Noah didn't still have one arm around her waist, her knees probably would've buckled. And if he was moving to Texas, she had the biggest decision of her life to make. Noah was everything she could ask for in a man and more. Being with him would mean always having Charlotte and Cheyenne in her life. And when he'd asked her the other day about having kids of her own, for the first time she'd wanted them, if it meant having Noah's child and adding to their blissful family.

THEY ARRIVED HOME shortly after ten. She wanted to stay out later but figured her parents were eager to be on their way. They checked on the girls together, watching them sleep peacefully. She fought every primal urge in her body to invite him back to her room so they could begin expanding their family. Her new feelings were unfamiliar to her and she wanted to make sure this was what she really wanted come the light of day.

They eased the door closed, facing each other in the darkened hallway. The single night-light near the floor cast an ethereal glow. Hannah lifted his shirt above the waistband of his jeans and splayed her fingers across his abdomen. As she slid them farther up his chest, his muscles tightened.

"What are you doing to me?" he groaned.

"I wanted to see if I had the same effect on you as you do on me." Hannah barely recognized her own voice. His skin was hot to her touch and she allowed her fingers to explore his body.

"You're about to find out just how much of an effect you have on me." He encircled her wrists with his hands. "You're driving me crazy. You don't understand the power you have over me. As much as I want to continue, we both should go to bed…regretfully alone."

She didn't want to let him go. Every inch of her skin begged for his touch. Every bit of her heart yearned for him to say the words she needed to hear—and yearned to say in return. She rose onto her toes and sought his mouth for one final kiss. "Sweet dreams, Noah."

She eased out of his arms and slipped into her room, closing the door behind her. If he knocked, she'd let him in. But she heard the click of his door shutting. Hannah slid down the door to the floor and drew her knees to her chest. A warmth coursed through her veins, settling deep within her.

"I think I just fell in love."

Chapter Twelve

Noah had always been an early riser, but he never would get used to going outside to collect eggs at five o'clock in the morning.

He'd basically asked Hannah to marry him last night. Not in so many words, though, for fear she'd say no. He knew she was still confused about Lauren and he respected her feelings. It was probably foolish of him to suggest marriage so soon, but they already had what most married people wanted after years together. He didn't see any reason to wait.

He fed the girls while Hannah attended to the horses. He had to leave for the airport in three hours and he missed them already. He felt like he was living two separate lives. Once he had everyone home in Oregon, then he would ask Hannah properly to marry him. That was, if she would go without a wedding ring on her finger. Noah laughed to himself. That was, if her family would let her. They were a very protective family and Noah loved that about them.

While Hannah was getting dressed after her shower,

his phone rang. He checked the caller ID and saw it was his real-estate agent.

"Hello, please tell me you have good news."

"I have great news. The ranch you saw last week is back on the market. I emailed you the listing again. The owners are anxious to sell, since they purchased a new place when they thought theirs had sold. They reduced the price. Look it over and let me know. If you want, we can put in an offer today."

Noah hung up the phone with increased hope. He ran upstairs to get his iPad and impatiently checked his email.

The listing photos didn't do it justice. The ranch was much more breathtaking in person. Twice the size of Hannah's with plenty of flat land for farming. The stables had been recently remodeled and it even had a henhouse, along with a few other penning areas for smaller animals. The house itself rivaled Hannah's in size but had numerous modern upgrades. The ranch was marketed as "new vintage," meaning it was a newer home meant to look turn-of-the-last-century. He couldn't wait for Hannah to come downstairs so he could show her.

While he waited, he decided to share with his little audience.

"What do you think?" Noah flipped through the pictures. "How would you like to live here?"

"How would they like to live where?" Hannah stood in the kitchen doorway.

"I just got off the phone with a real-estate agent." Noah handed her his iPad. "I heard about this ranch last week and went to see it. I had looked at others, but none were quite right. This one went back on the market today and I'm going to put an offer on it this afternoon. What do you think?"

Hannah stabbed at the iPad with her finger. "This is in Oregon."

"I know. I'm buying it for you and the girls." He slid closer to her and pointed to the picture with all the acreage. Look at all this farmland. Well, it will be farmland once you do whatever you have to do to it. Isn't it just perfect?"

"What do you mean you're buying a ranch in Oregon for me and the girls? I'm not moving to Oregon." Her face paled. "And neither are they."

"You don't understand." Noah took the iPad from her and continued to flip through the photos. "What's not to love? I made sure it had everything you wanted." He held up a picture of the stables. "These have been recently remodeled and have full height doors to prevent cribbing, whatever that means. They're—" he tilted his head side to side, not wanting to hurt her feelings "—they're an upgrade from what you have here. I'm sure your horses will appreciate it, not that there's anything wrong with your stables. And look here." He pointed to a large dirt enclosure. "There's an area big enough for you to practice. And here—" another photo appeared on the screen "—there are multiple pastures, plus twice the acreage you have here for you to farm. You can have a bigger organic farm than you dreamed."

Hannah ran her hands through her hair and paced the kitchen before she spun to face him. "I love how you just decided to move me and the twins away from my family. You completely disregarded my feelings. I cannot believe you just assumed I would be okay with this arrangement. You can't just dig up the soil, plant a few crops in the ground and call it an organic farm. We talked about this. A farm requires careful planning— Noah you have to plan your crops for the climate."

She lifted both the girls out of their high chairs and took them into the sunroom. Noah understood she was surprised, but he hadn't counted on this reaction. Even if she wasn't thrilled with the idea, he thought she'd at least take it into consideration.

"I did years of research before I decided what I was going to plant," she continued before entering the room. "My business plan took years of preparation. I can't just pick up and move the whole operation to Oregon. Not for nothing, but this is why I went through four years of college. If it were as easy as you make it sound, I wouldn't need a degree. The government has strict standards on what can be classified as USDA organic. Once you have everything else figured out, the physical land part is a three-year process. I'm already well into my first year. I can't believe you did this without discussing it with me. How could you?"

"Okay, so you have to start over again." Noah tried to hide his annoyance, but she made it impossible. "You bought this ranch in April, here it is December. Even if you started working the soil the day you bought it, you have at most eight months into it. And I'm sure it's probably more along the lines of seven. I went out of my way to find something you would love. This isn't for me. I think it's a little selfish for you to turn it down without even flying out to see it."

"I'm selfish?" She glared at him with reproach. "I think you need to take a good look in the mirror. When you were talking about making this permanent, I thought you meant you were moving here. You're not thinking of me or the girls. You're thinking only about yourself. You—" she pointed at him "—came into our lives. You want to uproot me, the children and my family for you."

His mind whirled at her remark. "How am I uprooting your family?"

"Because you're asking me to leave the people I love. They're still going to want to be a part of the girls' lives. In order to do that, they'd have to come visit us." She threw her hands in the air. "You're asking everyone to make allowances for you. Just so you can keep your job. You have no regard for me or my job." She slapped her chest. "I have responsibilities here. I have the farm, I have the rodeo school, the horses I train and board. Let alone my professional career as a barrel racer. I'm not ready to retire yet."

"I'm not asking you to."

"In a way you are. When I race, I have a support system that helps me with the girls. We won't have that in Oregon. Is your mom going to drop everything every time I go on the road? And if my parents aren't available, my brother and sister-in-law are. The only person you're thinking about is yourself."

"How can you tell me I'm selfish when everything I'm doing is for you and the girls?" Noah felt his blood pumping through his veins. "I built my house—my dream house—spent years designing it, and I'm selling it so you and the girls can have a place to live with every amenity you're accustomed to and then some." Noah stormed to the front of the house. "I can't believe you're disregarding it without even seeing it. You haven't even visited Oregon yet. How can you say if you like it or not?"

Hannah flattened her palm against her mouth and breathed deeply. "This isn't about me liking it or not." Her tone softened slightly. "It's about you trying to make the decision for us. It's not our home."

"They're twenty-two months old. They will adjust. Chances are they won't even remember this place when they grow up."

Hannah grabbed a hold of the banister. "Just like they won't remember their mother."

"No, they probably won't." Noah hated to hurt her. "That's the sad reality. I know that's not what you want to hear, but unfortunately, they probably won't remember Lauren. All we can do is keep her memory alive and that's all you because I don't have anything to share with them. I don't want to do this without you."

"You never gave me the respect of even discussing it with me." Hannah lowered herself onto the second to last step. "Was this ranch what last night was all about?"

Noah stared down at the floor. "Part of it. The other part was because I want to solidify us as a family. In order to do so, I had to have a place for us all to live. My house sits atop a steep bank overlooking the Willamette River. I don't have a backyard for the girls to play in. It's a beautiful home, private and secluded, but I don't think the girls would be happy there. I know you wouldn't be."

"You have the perfect solution to all your problems right in front of you. You're standing in it. But it's all about you and your job." She rose, rubbing her palms against the front of her jeans. "I can't believe this is happening. Only a few hours ago I was falling in love with you, dreaming of our future together. You've completely crushed all of it, casting my life, my family and my feelings aside as if they don't matter. I can't love a man who doesn't respect me. Whatever we had, it's over. The girls and I are going to my parents' house. Please be gone by the time we return."

Noah watched Hannah drive away from the house. At least she'd granted him the courtesy of saying goodbye to his daughters. They hadn't cried or even been upset, probably because they expected to see him soon enough. What happens now? Would Hannah even allow him to video chat with his daughters? None of this was necessary. All she had to do was say yes.

He hadn't expected her to throw him a parade, but he thought she would have at least considered the idea. She barely acknowledged the photos. If she cared anything about him and their future together, she would have opened her mind to the idea.

God, it hurt. It hurt that she could so decidedly end their relationship over a ranch.

He loved her. *Loved.* What the hell was love anyway?

Noah stormed up the stairs to his room and jammed his belongings in his duffel. The sooner he was away from Hannah, the better. He halted in the doorway, staring across the hall at the empty cribs. They had been so close to being a real family.

Noah locked the front door behind him and tucked the key in the horse-head wreath. He sent Hannah a one-line text telling her where he'd left it, then slid behind the wheel of his rental and started the engine. He drove to the edge of the property and glanced at the house in the rearview mirror. Almost a month ago he'd driven down this road for the first time. Now he didn't know when or if he'd ever see it again.

Leaving Ramblewood meant leaving Charlotte and Cheyenne. They wouldn't stay separated for long. Hannah may not want to move to Oregon, but that wouldn't stop him from getting custody of his daughters. She could visit. He would never keep her from the girls or vice versa. He wouldn't be that cruel. He only prayed she'd grant him the same courtesy in the meantime.

THE FOLLOWING MORNING, Hannah scheduled an emergency meeting with Avery. After her breakup with Noah, she needed to know her rights and her options.

"I can't believe he did this." Hannah paced the length of Avery's office.

Avery removed her glasses and set them on the desk. "Honestly, Hannah, I find it rather touching that he was willing to go through all that trouble for you."

"You can't be serious," Hannah scoffed. "He admitted his house wasn't suitable for the girls. This has nothing to do with me. He's failed to consider my feelings since day one. He had no intention of moving here."

"If he didn't respect you, he wouldn't have chosen to look for a house you would like. Something that suited your needs. Not his and not the girls. They could live in a condo. This was very much about you."

"But he didn't discuss it with me." Hannah's jaw ached from clenching it. "He didn't take into account my feelings about leaving my family and friends behind."

Avery rose and walked around the front of her desk. "Did you take his into account?"

"What?" Hannah shook her head. It wasn't about him, it was about the girls.

"You told me from the very beginning the girls needed to stay here. Did you give any thought to moving to Oregon?"

"He asked me once."

"And what did you say?"

Hannah sighed. "I got mad."

"But he attempted to discuss the situation?"

She laughed nervously. "Am I on the witness stand?"

"That wasn't my point, but you need to realize if this goes to court because you two couldn't work out a successful resolution, you will have to answer similar questions. Right now, I'm trying to be your friend. Did you ever consider moving to Oregon?"

"No. It's not that simple. I have a life here."

"I'm willing to bet Noah has a life in Oregon, too."

"What about the allowances I made for Noah while he was here?" Surely they had to count in her favor. She'd opened up her home to the man.

"If this does go to court, that will be taken into consideration, but it could work against you, too. You allowed a man you didn't know to move into your home."

Shock flew through her. "My brother did a background check on him."

"Just because someone hasn't been caught committing a crime doesn't mean a crime hasn't been committed." Avery waved her hands. "I'm not saying he's guilty of anything, I'm saying a judge may very well question your decision making. I really wish you had consulted me first or even told me he was staying with you. The sentiment was lovely, but I would have strongly advised against it."

"I'm going to lose, aren't I?" Icy fear coiled around her heart.

"You might." Avery squeezed Hannah's hands. "Noah has a strong case. He can prove he was willing to make concessions in order for you to live with him and the girls. Offering to buy you a ranch is huge. He went above and beyond reasonable expectations in order for you to be comfortable and to give you a similar home to what you have here. His attorney may ask him if he would've considered moving to Ramblewood if his job hadn't been a factor."

"He could've changed his job."

"You could have, too. You're accusing Noah of not respecting your feelings or your job. Aren't you doing the same thing?"

Hannah didn't like being wrong. Maybe she had been selfish. He made more money. And even if she had an extremely good year racing, it still wouldn't match what he made. But money shouldn't be the only factor. "My family is here. The girls' family."

"And his mother is there," Avery stated. "The girls have another grandparent they haven't met yet. I'm sure she'll want to be a part of their lives."

Hannah pressed her hands against the side of her head. "There has to be a compromise."

Avery smiled tightly. "I think Noah already offered you a compromise. Your education taught you organic farming beyond the Texas border. I realize you were specializing in regional produce, but you're intelligent. With some more planning, you can do the same thing up there. You won't have the extended growing season, but maybe you can tweak your business plan and plant some indoor crops. You have even more options when it comes to the work you do with horses. And you could still compete from Oregon. It wouldn't be as convenient, but you could do it. Noah doesn't have any of that flexibility as a heli-logger."

"I wish you would stop making sense."

"Unfortunately, making sense is my job."

HANNAH SPENT THE majority of the night researching the ranch Noah had found in Oregon. Since there wasn't a rodeo school nearby, she'd be forced to rely solely on organic farming. She might have the opportunity to train barrel horses after she built a reputation in the area, but that would require her buying the horses herself, training and then selling them. It was time consuming and less than lucrative. Boarding horses was still an option, but again, without a reputation, she would have to offer rock-bottom rates in order to gain a clientele.

There were three similar organic farms within a five-mile radius of where Noah wanted to move. Competition would be steep, plus she would have to wait three years until her farm would be certified organic. The location near the pacific rainforest would definitely require her to rethink her crops. She had studied, pored over her books and lost sleep thinking about crops specifically for the Hill Country region of Texas. Now Noah was asking her to throw it all away. She didn't know how to throw away four years. She slammed her laptop closed. She appreciated the effort he'd put into finding her a ranch—a pretty good ranch, but she couldn't get past her pain. Noah hadn't respected her enough to discuss their future with her, and that hurt. It really hurt.

Chapter Thirteen

Christmas was in three days and Hannah couldn't get Noah out of her head…or her heart. The children had been asking for him. Actually asking for Daddy. Of course, they had to start that after he'd left for Oregon. Hannah still spoke to him every day, but only long enough to set up the video chat for the girls. She may be hurt and upset with him, but she would never cut him out of their lives. Noah's flight was due around nine tonight, and Hannah had told him to book a hotel room. Her mother had been livid when she'd found out and had invited Noah to stay with them, but he didn't want to come between them at Christmastime and had declined. At least he had considered her feelings that time.

Avery had called earlier in the day and given her their court date. It was the Monday after New Year's and Noah was staying in town until then. They had each asked for sole custody but had allowed the other visitation. Hannah had begun having nightmares about losing the children and Avery had done her best to prepare her in case it happened. She repeatedly urged Hannah to try to work things out with Noah, but Hannah didn't feel that would be fair to any of them. How could she love a man she had no business loving in the first place? And what example would she be setting for Charlotte and Cheyenne if she sacrificed her life and happiness for a man? One question had plagued her every night since Noah left. Would living with him in Oregon have been that much of a sacrifice? The ranch he'd shown her was still for sale and she'd looked at it a few times. Okay, every day. Maybe ten times a day. The stables were nicer, and she wouldn't mind a house with newer plumbing and more than one bathroom. It had many of the upgrades she had eventually intended to do on the farmhouse and the exterior was a soft yellow… Lauren's color.

But the more Hannah thought about it, the less she could imagine herself in Oregon. She had a hard time believing Noah had really loved her for herself and not just the girls. He may have thought it was love, but he was only fooling himself. It had been easy to get caught up in the moment, especially where Charlotte and Cheyenne were concerned. Staying together would have been the easiest option. And maybe there was some genuine attraction on his part, but she doubted he would have taken such a big step so early on if it weren't for the girls.

A tear rolled down her cheek. She missed her best friend more than anything. Whenever she'd had a problem, she'd always turned to Lauren. She'd never felt more alone, even with her family around her. She didn't know what she would do if she lost the girls. A nagging voice kept telling her Lauren would've wished for her happiness regardless of where she lived or whom she lived with. She wanted to be with Noah, but only if he truly wanted her, too.

NOAH HAD SPENT three of the last four days preparing for his looming court date. His company had secured the heli-logger from British Columbia, affording him more time off. His attorney had managed to get him a home inspection…at his mother's house. The location of Noah's house was just too dangerous. It hadn't mattered anyway. He'd listed it for sale on Monday. It hadn't been as painful as he'd expected. Material items held very little value to him now that Charlotte and Cheyenne were in his life. But it felt empty. He saw Hannah's face on his phone every day, but he missed her smile. He missed her laugh and he missed laughing with her.

He'd been able to catch an earlier flight to Texas, anxious to be in the same town as his girls. His heart was heavy with the memory of what was. The excitement was gone. He still looked forward to seeing his daughters, but it wasn't the same. He wouldn't be waking them up, feeding them or dressing them. Instead, he would be allowed to swing by for a couple hours to visit with his children. It wasn't what he would call quality time.

Noah stuffed his bag in the overhead bin and took his seat near the window. Hannah had said he was selfish. Maybe she was right. He hadn't considered her jobs. He tended to be on the hubristic side, thanks to his time in the air force and his career. He was used to being special, but in reality he was no more special than anybody else, regardless of what he did for a living. Spending time with Hannah had humbled him in many ways. Unfortunately, the lesson hit home a little too late.

The seat belt sign flashed and the flight attendant began her speech. By the end of the day he'd be holding his daughters in his arms. He never wanted to let them go again. Leaving the last time had been too painful. He had a sinking feeling the judge would grant Hannah custody of his daughters. His attorney was hopeful but had warned him that character references may come into play, and Hannah had the entire town of Ramblewood on her side. His friends and coworkers would vouch for him without question. His mom was another story. She felt Noah had been inflexible and had overstepped when it came to wanting to move the girls to Oregon. She'd added more validity to Hannah's argument by reiterating that Charlotte and Cheyenne would be in day care most of the day if they lived with him, versus being surrounded by family and friends in Texas. She also reminded him that she had worked multiple jobs to support him when he was a kid and then asked how he would have felt if a stranger had come in and ripped him from the only home he knew. The plane taxied down the runway, picking up speed. He gripped the arms of the seat. He may be one of the top helicopter pilots in the world, but he was a horrible passenger. He hated not being in control.

Noah had made a big mistake. He could have looked into other job options and he hadn't. There was a helicopter flight school an hour from Hannah. Since he planned to be in town over the holidays, he'd gone ahead and set up a job interview with them. He'd taught a few seminars there over the years and he might have the opportunity to train future heli-loggers at their location. It was a compromise he was willing to make for the sake of his girls…all three of them. He wasn't willing to take the chance of losing them. He would leave everything behind in order for them to stay a family.

HANNAH WATCHED THE CLOCK. Noah's plane was scheduled to land in two hours. She didn't want him to stay in a hotel over Christmas and New Year's. She wanted him here with her and the girls. She owed it to them to give her relationship with Noah one last try before they went to court. One way or another, she needed to know if they truly loved each other.

Hannah picked up the phone and dialed her brother. "Would you mind if I borrowed your truck tonight?"

"Only if it's for a worthy cause."

She rolled her eyes. Somewhere along the line, Clay had become a Noah supporter and he'd given her a hard time ever since she told Noah to leave last Sunday.

"It's for a good cause."

"Are you taking the girls with you?" he asked. "Or do you need Abby and me to babysit for you?"

"Normally I wouldn't bring them, but *Daddy* is their new favorite word. And I know how much it would mean to him to see them right when he gets off the plane. Maybe it will help soften my decision."

"You finally came to your senses?" he teased.

"If I didn't know better, I would say you're trying to get rid of me. And my decision has conditions."

"I just want you to be happy, sis. Give me a few minutes and I'll be over. You can drop me back off on your way out."

"Girls?" Hannah walked into the living room, where Charlotte and Cheyenne were playing in the middle of the floor. "How would you two like to see Daddy?"

Cheyenne rose to her feet with the aid of her sister's head and toddled over to her. "I see Daddy."

Hannah knelt on the floor in front of her. "You'll see Daddy once you get dressed."

Charlotte's face lit up brighter than the Christmas tree. "Daddy!" Hannah held out her arms for Charlotte, feeling more confident than ever she was making the right decision. She belonged with Noah, even if that meant moving to Oregon. "Daddy!" Charlotte toddled past her and into the foyer. Hannah turned to catch her, and that was when she saw him.

"Hello, beautiful."

"Noah!" Hannah's hand flew to her chest. "How did you— Where did you—"

"I took an earlier flight and the key I left in your wreath was still there." Noah crouched as his daughters ran to him. He attempted to scoop them into his arms, only to be tackled backward onto the floor. His laugh echoed through the foyer and the entire house.

"Look, girls, Daddy's home."

Noah sat upright. "Am I home? Because I'd really like to be."

Hannah covered her face with her hands. "What are you saying? I thought you wanted us to come to Oregon."

Noah shook his head. "Oregon isn't for you. You

would never be happy there. Your home isn't just composed of four walls and some land. It's made up of friends and family, too. This is your home."

"Are you saying you could be happy here?" She attempted to make sense of his words. "What about your job?"

"I could be happy anywhere you and the girls are." He gave each of the twins a kiss on the cheek, causing them to squeal in delight.

Hannah slowly rose to her feet and offered Noah help up. He took her hand and knelt before her. Laughing, Hannah kept pulling on him to stand, but Noah wouldn't move.

She looked down at him, trying to register the significance of his posture. He was on one knee.

"Noah, don't tease me." He couldn't possibly be proposing after all the crap they'd been through.

He removed a black velvet box from his pocket and lifted the lid.

Hannah's heart lurched as her pulse leaped with excitement. "Noah." A knot rose in her throat.

"Your mom asked me the morning of the pancake brunch if I was in love with you. And I couldn't answer her, because even though I thought I knew what love felt like, being with you was unlike any other feeling I'd ever experienced. Every emotion, every sensation is heightened and exciting when I'm around you. These past few days have been the worst days of my life. I need you by my side. I love you, Hannah Tanner. Will you do me the honor of becoming my wife…in Texas?"

She knelt before him and wrapped her arms around

Charlotte and Cheyenne. "What do you two think? Should I marry Daddy?"

"I love Daddy," Cheyenne said.

Hannah's eyes met his. "I love your daddy, too, very much."

"Is that a yes?" he asked.

Hannah nodded, words escaping her and tears streaming down her cheeks.

Noah slipped the ring on her finger and eased her to her feet. "I love you, Hannah."

"And I love you, Noah Knight. Now and forever."

Epilogue

Three days later, on Christmas morning, Noah and Hannah joined Charlotte and Cheyenne around the Christmas tree, opening gifts. Noah had fully supported Hannah's decision to wrap and give the girls the presents from Lauren. Neither one of them had been sure how the twins would react when they heard who they were from, but they handled it better than expected. Noah was quickly learning how resilient children were. They amazed him more each day.

Noah's mother had caught a last-minute flight, eager to meet her grandbabies and join them and Hannah's family for Christmas. Every time he looked at his expanded family, he learned something new. He couldn't imagine his world without them. Hannah and the twins were the best gifts he'd ever received.

Later that evening, Noah waited on Hannah's front porch for his bride. His mother stood by his side as his precious Charlotte and Cheyenne tossed red rose petals around the porch, Abby attempting to keep the flowers out of their little mouths.

Some might call him crazy for wanting to make it

official so soon. He may have even said the same if he were on the outside looking in. He hadn't known a love like this could exist, and once he had, he couldn't let it go.

The front door swung open. Hannah, escorted by her father, stepped out wearing a long-sleeve, cream-colored ruffled lace gown. It was country, it was beautiful and it was 100 percent Hannah.

His heart danced in his chest every time he looked at his family. Thirty-five days ago, he hadn't known they existed. As they said their "I dos" before their friends and family, a single star shot across the sky…a Christmas gift from above.

Noah wrapped his arms around all three of his girls and held them close.

"Merry Christmas!"

* * * * *

#1625 HER COLORADO SHERIFF

Rocky Mountain Twins • by Patricia Thayer

Newly hired as interim sheriff of Hidden Springs, Colorado, Cullen Brannigan plans to move into a house on the family ranch...except he finds it's already occupied by Shelby Townsend and her five-year-old nephew!

#1626 A VALENTINE FOR THE COWBOY

Sapphire Mountain Cowboys
by Rebecca Winters

Rancher Eli Clayton is raising his little fourteen-month-old daughter, Libby. When he sees her happily ensconced in the arms of a beautiful stranger, he begins to wonder if his daughter needs a mommy...and if he needs a wife!

#1627 THE BULL RIDER'S COWGIRL

Men of Raintree Ranch • by April Arrington

When easy-living bull rider Colt Mead becomes his young sister's guardian, he needs Jen Taylor's help. But it will take more than friendship to convince the determined barrel racer to give up her race for glory.

#1628 RODEO FATHER

by Mary Sullivan

Cowboy Travis Read has always been a loner. But when he meets Rachel McGuire, the pregnant widow and her daughter make him believe being part of a family might be possible after all!

———————

HWESTCNM1216

REQUEST YOUR FREE BOOKS!
2 FREE NOVELS PLUS 2 FREE GIFTS!

ᕼ HARLEQUIN®

ᗯestern ᖇomance

ROMANCE THE ALL-AMERICAN WAY!

Hearing the feminine voice, Cullen swung around to find
Shelby standing in the doorway. She looked fresh and
pretty dressed in her jeans and blouse. Her rich brown
hair was pulled back into a ponytail. She was ready for
work at the café.

"Sorry, I knocked, and I heard you…" She paused. "I
just wanted to tell you that… Never mind." She frowned.
"I can see that this isn't a good time. I'll come back later."

When she started to leave, he hurried after her. "Wait."
He caught her hand. "Don't go, Shelby. It's not you. In
fact, you're just what I need right now." When he tugged
on her hand it caused her to stumble right into his arms.
He saw her surprise, her rapid breathing, but more than
that, those eyes, blue depths, held passion. And he wanted
her.

"Cullen?"

Her saying his name broke the last of his resistance.
He lowered his head and brushed his lips across hers. He
was quickly becoming lost. His mouth moved over hers

gently, and when she didn't resist, he wrapped his arms around her and held her close.

Oh, God. She felt wonderful. Her taste, her softness and that sexy body… He tilted her head, getting a better angle to deepen the kiss. She moaned and her hands moved to his chest, and he burned. He wanted more. He cupped her face and kissed her deeper. Then reluctantly, he ended the kiss and released her. He watched her blink those startling blue eyes, and he almost went back for more. Instead he slipped his hands into his pockets and said, "Wow! I didn't mean to do that… Did you want to ask me something?"

She opened her mouth and paused as if to clear her head. "Huh, I just was going to offer to help you with the horses." She couldn't look him in the eyes. "Look, I should go. Ryan's in the car."

He started to argue, then stopped. "Okay."

She nodded. "I'll see you later." She turned and walked out the back door. He watched her until she got into her car and drove off.

"Well, that was just great, Brannigan. Talk about overstepping your boundaries."

How was he going to fix this?

Don't miss
HER COLORADO SHERIFF by Patricia Thayer,
available January 2017 wherever
Harlequin® Western Romance®
books and ebooks are sold.

www.Harlequin.com

Love the Harlequin book you just read?

Your opinion matters.

Review this book on your favorite
book site, review site, blog or your own
social media properties and share
your opinion with other readers!

JUST CAN'T GET ENOUGH?

Join our social communities
and talk to us online.

You will have access to the latest
news on upcoming titles and special
promotions, but most importantly,
you can talk to other fans about your
favorite Harlequin reads.

Harlequin.com/Community

Facebook.com/HarlequinBooks

Twitter.com/HarlequinBooks

Pinterest.com/HarlequinBooks